A WILD OLD MAN ON THE ROAD

Other books by Morley Callaghan:

Strange Fugitive (1928)
An Autumn Penitent (1929)
A Native Argosy (1929)
It's Never Over (1930)
Broken Journey (1932)
Such Is My Beloved (1934)
They Shall Inherit the Earth (1935)
Now That April's Here (1936)
More Joy in Heaven (1937)
The Varsity Story (1945)
Luke Baldwin's Vow (1949)
The Loved and the Lost (1951)
The Many Colored Coat (1960)
A Passion in Rome (1961)
That Summer in Paris (1963)
A Fine and Private Place (1975)
Season of the Witch (1976)
Close to the Sun Again (1977)
No Man's Meat and The Enchanted Pimp (1978)
A Time for Judas (1983)
Our Lady of the Snows (1985)
The Lost and Found Stories (1985)

MORLEY CALLAGHAN

A WILD OLD MAN ON THE ROAD

Stoddart

First published in 1988 by
Stoddart Publishing Co. Limited
34 Lesmill Road
Toronto, Canada
M3B 2T6

Canadian Cataloguing in Publication Data

Callaghan, Morley, 1903-
  A wild old man on the road

ISBN 0-7737-2192-4

1. Title.

PS8505.A43W54 1988   C813'.52   C88-093088-8
PR9199.3.C343W54 1988

TEXT DESIGN: Brant Cowie/ArtPlus Limited
TYPE OUTPUT: Tony Gordon Ltd.

Printed and bound in the United States

For Miranda
My reader yet to be

MARK DIDION CAME TO Paris and took a room in the Continental Hotel with a window overlooking the Seine. A blue-eyed young man of medium height in blue jeans, fawn-coloured jacket, red shirt open at the throat, dark brown hair a little too long, and a confident air, he was the son of the recently deceased Andrew Didion, the president of a large advertising agency that held many government contracts. He came there late in the summer, just months after the frightening student riots that had demoralized Paris. In other great cities, too, there had been riots and bombings. It was a time of freedom marches and peace parades and songs of liberation. A lot of people felt good. In the United States the blacks had had their own great freedom marches. While the Vietnam War went on and on, young men and women marched for peace.

On his own, Mark would never have chosen the expensive Hilton Continental, but he knew that if his father had lived and been there with him, he would, in his opulent manner, have insisted they stay at a grand hotel; he would have liked the room they gave him. From that window, Paris, shimmering in the late sunlight, now looked as peaceful as it must have looked to his father forty years ago. There on the river in the valley between great rows of old apartment buildings, all with mansard roofs, was the excursion boat on its way to St Cloude, soon to pass Île de la Cité, and below, a little to the left, the Louvre, and almost directly ahead, the bridge to the Left Bank.

Then, as the red sun vanished, the light of the river changed. Feeling restless, Mark went down to the bar, had a drink, then sauntered around the lobby getting the feel of the place. He saw three young Europeans dressed just as he was except that he had on a red shirt. Fluent in French, he asked a girl at the desk where the Café de la Paix was. Nearby, she said, less than a ten-minute walk. It was the café where his father, according to the diary, went for his first meal on his first day in Paris. Leaving the hotel, he found the old café. Many Americans and middle-aged women were on the terrace. He went inside and had an expensive supper of pheasant with morels and a bottle of Chambertin which he nursed for a long time, trying to relax and free himself from an unfamiliar sense of expectancy. Soon the wine, after the long flight on the plane, began to make him feel woozy, so he left the café. The night air cleared his head. Looking around, feeling strangely happy, he wandered over to the Madeleine and a movie theatre showing the American comic, Jerry Lewis; there was a lineup a block long. Paris and Jerry Lewis!

Back in his hotel room, stretching out on the bed, he dozed. Suddenly awake, he got up and stood again at the window looking across the river. Somewhere over there on the Left Bank was the little hotel where his father, as a young man, had lived. Now he could imagine standing beside him, their heads close together, his six-foot father two inches taller, and with his clipped grey moustache, balding head and cynical light-blue eyes, saying, "Yes, Mark. Over there. A good long walk up from the river. Raspail and the boulevard du Montparnasse." He imagined himself questioning his father and getting answers. They said things to each other, surprising and interesting things they could never have said while

Andrew Didion was alive and they were living in the big house in Toronto's moneyed Rosedale ravine.

It was a thirteen-roomed gabled brick house, lavishly restored and now done in white stucco, the property enclosed by a high wooden fence. Heavy vines hung on the house and the chimneys. In the spring, flowing wisteria covered the whole front of the house. While Mark was an undergraduate at University College, he had big parties and on such nights his father felt compelled to get out. He disapproved of Mark's friends. He had contempt for the way the men and women dressed — the men in torn jeans and sneakers or desert boots, the women in long dowdy clothes or sometimes half naked. "It's a uniform," he jeered. "They're all in uniform, and my God, they don't even know it." But Mark's mother, a quiet dark slim gracious woman, seemed to enjoy these parties that often lasted till dawn. She had a serenity and dignity that had so impressed the neighbours they found it difficult to complain about the parties. If singing till dawn was all right with her, then it ought to be acceptable to the neighbours, she seemed to be saying with her distinguished air. Old Mrs. Walton, a neighbour who was easily outraged, did go so far as to say to Mark's mother, though smiling as she said it, "I happened to wake up at dawn. It was nice lying there for hours listening to the singing." After the parties, the house reeked of the sweet smell of marijuana.

Trying to be good-humoured, Andrew Didion once said, "Your fervent socialism, I can understand, Mark. The young take a shot at socialism as they used to take a shot at going to Sunday school. But your crowd! Why are they all tarred with the same brush? The men dress like bums, the girls talk like truck drivers, and you all hug each other. Why all this witless hugging — all out in the open? Is it something in the air?"

Holding his temper, Mark said, "All right, Dad. It's not your time. It's my time. It's a wonderful time to be alive.

You'll just have to take my word for it. You'll never know."
He laughed because he thought he knew what his father
stood for: he was an arch-conservative; no, more than that, a
pigheaded flamboyant conservative burdened with a socialist
son, and still getting his suits from Saville Row in London.
Though he had the patrician manner, he had a lyrical grasp
of all the four-letter words and could use them freely on
Cabinet ministers and friends in high places. In his business,
he knew how to protect himself in his ruthless competitive
fashion. On weekends he wore jackets and Ascot ties and
played a good game of tennis. He rode to hounds with his
friends in the country who all had their own hunts, and yet,
as Mark learned from his mother, he was secretly worried by
the smell of marijuana in the house after a party.

Sometimes coming along the street long past midnight,
after an evening at the Barclay Hotel where he had been
courting the enchanting Hungarian dancer, Marika, Mark
would weave a little, or stand still to get his balance, or
sometimes sit down for a while on a lawn waiting for his
head to clear. At this hour on his street, all the lights would
be out, all but the one in his father's room. As he looked a
long time at that light, he was aware that no matter how late
it was, the light would be there, until he opened the front
door, his father waiting to hear the door close. Only then
would he turn off his light. Nothing was ever said. Mark
wasn't a user. Sometimes he would smoke a joint just to be
sociable, but even then he didn't like the silly look that came
so often on the faces of his smoking friends. But aside from
this, he had been profoundly shaken by the death of his close
friend, Mat Drillon. His father knew about Mat; he had met
him at the parties. Mat liked reciting poetry. He was a
medieval scholar, a loveable bright handsome man who took
LSD and believed that in his time the lost world of the dream
and the hallucination was being recovered. One night he
drove his car down to the waterfront, parked facing the lake

and blew his brains out. Finally, Mark said to his father, "Look Dad, it's hard to talk to you about anything; we don't speak the same language. But I want you to know I'm not into drugs!"

"Thank you, Mark," he said stiffly. But late at night the light still remained in his window till the front door was opened and closed.

Believing that Mark would take a job in the agency after he had finished his undergraduate studies, Andrew Didion had him come to the office and meet the junior executives. That summer he paid for him to cross the country, see the prairie cities and go on to Vancouver. Then Mark fooled him. In the fall, supported by his mother, Mark went to graduate school and there, working on his thesis on Albert Camus, he kept his dream of becoming a journalist to himself. At that time, the personal journalist was in high fashion. These men and women, whether writing about political conventions, freedom marches or prize fights, made their own impressions and reflections more important than the story they covered. The one journalist Mark studied and revered was the English man of letters, Jeremy Monk, who had written about Chaucer, Joseph Conrad, his own time in Montparnasse in Paris, and the great book on his days with the Republicans in the Spanish Civil War. But Monk was out of step with the new journalists; he did not go on lecture tours or advertise himself; at best, he was a revered cult figure concerned only with truthful reporting.

In the vacation summer of his second year at graduate school, Mark went to Quebec and lived with a French family; he became utterly at ease in their language. He could think in French; he could dream in French. So immersed was he in this literature he loved that characters in French fiction — Balzac's Rastignac, Flaubert's Emma, Zola's Nana or

Proust's Swann — were more real and closer to him than some people he met every day. He had read all the books about Montparnasse in the twenties. In his imagination he could see the cafés: La Coupole, Le Sélect, La Closerie des Lilas. He could see himself sitting there with André Gide or Jean Cocteau, or a fictional character just as real to him — Bubu of Montparnasse. They were all in his head and alive for him. Moreover, it had excited him to discover that Jeremy Monk was the first one to point out that the new sense of personal freedom, the liberation of the spirit and of the person, had been apparent all around him in the artists of the twenties. In his notebook Mark wrote: "Our time really began back there." That night he lay daydreaming about Jeremy Monk coming to America, then Canada, and in the daydream, he was the one who made the speech introducing him to the big audience at Convocation Hall.

But before the end of that summer he had to hurry home. His mother died after only a month's illness from cancer of the liver. She had been his friend. He never talked about his mother, yet she seemed to be always with him. Now, he and his father, alone in the big house with the Filipina housekeeper, shied away from each other; they bickered and wrangled. Everything they did together, the necessary things around the house, everything happening in the world outside the house, became an irritant. While his mother was alive, Mark, studying in his room, had played records. All night long, he played the blues records of blind Ray Charles and no one complained. After his mother's death, his father would yell, "You're driving me crazy. Shut it off, do you hear?"

Mark told himself it was time to be rid of his father. Day by day, he got ready to be rid of him, and yet one night in the last week of his days at graduate school when his father, having dinner, asked him to stay in and talk with the guests, young advertising men, he listened to a general conversation about psychoanalysis. It was fashionable for a hard-driving young executive in the creative department to have an analyst. Mark, listening, was filled with astonishment. His father was talking about art and Freud. "Ah, yes," he said. "When I was twenty-two I was carried away by Freud's dream book. Dreams. Dreams. Freud even made up dreams and interpreted them. That was the key for me. Yes, we all need dreams. But it was when I was studying Freud's case books I got the hang of him. What you don't understand is that Freud is a storyteller. A great storyteller. His cases are his stories, all carefully crafted. He's really a great artist. Why don't you try looking at him in that way?" To Mark he sounded so much more interesting than his colleagues. Feeling that he had caught a glimpse of a man he had never known, he felt baffled, then cheated. Leaving the dinner party, he went down to the Barclay to catch the last show and have Marika take him home with her, and she did. But she was a European who knew how to let him just sample her sensual treasures while she waited for him to show he could get hold of some of his father's money.

Though it was very late when he got home he went right up to his father's room, opened the door and in the dark, and hardly able to see his father there apparently asleep on the bed, he said angrily, "You just turned out the light. What is this, for god's sake? From now on go to sleep when you go to bed. What do you think you're waiting for?" He didn't know why he was angry. His father didn't stir. Nothing more was said, nothing was to be said till the night of the big Hart House debate when Mark was a principal speaker. Whenever there was one of these college debates and there was a distinguished visiting speaker — this time the American academic, Gerald McNiece from Washington to defend the American intervention in Vietnam — the House invited city dignitaries, politicians and editors. Harold Hines, the managing editor of *The Star*, attended with Mark's father. Hines, a tall thin man with sad eyes and an ascetic air, was a drinking companion of Andrew Didion. Mark made a good speech. He could get really worked up about the Vietnam War. He was witty in the beginning, then becoming harsher, he made a slashing attack on the imperial American effort to dominate Southeast Asia. After the debate, when they were all having coffee in the Warden's room, Harold Hines said to Mark, "Just as bold and firm-minded as your father, eh Mark? Well, I'd like to have a copy of that speech. Where did you learn to talk or write like that?"

"I don't know. Reading, I suppose," Mark said.

"It's a good straightforward style, clear and cool," Hines said. "I think you'd do well in journalism."

"He'll also do well in the advertising business. Let him be, Harold," Andrew Didion said.

"He has the ability to analyze a complex situation in a straightforward simple style. That's a rare gift, Andrew." And turning to Mark, he said, "Have you thought of journalism, Mark?"

"Yes, I have, Mr. Hines. I've often thought about it."

"Right now I'd like to give you some freelance assignments and see how you do. If it works out, I think we might be able to find a place for you."

"Don't waste your time, Harold," Andrew Didion said. "Mark is coming into the agency with me. We'll find a place for him."

"Well, as they say, Mr. Hines, Father knows best," Mark said sourly.

When they got home and were sitting in the library facing each other, Mark said, "You can see I'm not like you, Dad."

"Of course not, Mark."

"I don't want to be like you."

"That's out of our hands. And by the way, since Hines asked, who is your guru?"

"I haven't got a guru."

"Some Cambridge communist, I gather from your speech. Well, with me when I was at college, it used to be H.L. Mencken. Who reads Mencken now?"

"Look, Dad, I'm definitely not going into your agency."

"No, well, I'm definitely going to bed. Good night," he said.

In the morning Mark went to the newspaper office and told Harold Hines he was finished at the graduate school and looking for a job. "Great, Mark," Hines said. "Now let me tell you how we'll do this." All men coming to work on this paper had first gained experience on out-of-town papers, he said. He would look around and find Mark a spot on a small-town paper where he could stay for six months, then he could fit in here and feel at home. "I'll be in touch with you in a week," he said, and Mark, hiding his disappointment, went home.

That night after dinner he was in the library reading a book by the beautiful Italian journalist, Renata. It was a story of a tormented love affair with Jeremy Monk that began in Paris in Montparnasse where Monk lived, and ended on one of the Greek islands. Renata wrote that it broke her heart remembering the lovely days in Montparnasse where they had known all the writers, the waiters, the painters and the dance halls, and where she had found a magic that came from Monk's kind of sensuality. Delight came to all her senses not only from the way he touched her, but when she walked with him in little parks, or looked at clothes, or watching the heavy shadows under the chestnut trees with the Luxembourg all in sunlight. When with him, everything was always in high bright colours, and she delighted in being a woman.

Looking up from his reading, he saw his father standing at the door, frowning, watching him with a baffled curiosity. On impulse Mark blurted out, "How about giving me the money for a trip to Paris?"

"Paris?" he said, startled. "Why Paris?"

"A young man, they say, should go to Paris."

"So they used to say."

"At my age you went to Paris, didn't you?"

"It got me a job in the creative department of the agency. What's it going to get you?"

"Will you give me the money?"

"Of course not. A young man should make his own way to Paris."

"Then maybe I will."

"Well, you're on your own now," and he smiled. Then, as he was leaving, "Don't forget to let them know you're coming."

"Leave it to me," Mark said belligerently. "Just leave everything to me," and for a while, nursing his hostility, he thought about taking the two thousand dollars his mother had left him and spending it on a week in Paris. Then cooling down, he realized he would need that bit of money if he went to work on a small-town paper. For six months he certainly wouldn't get any help from his father. This happened on a Wednesday night. On the Friday of that week his father had the stroke that paralyzed his left side and left him dying in the hospital.

Alone in the big house Mark had a nervous, jumpy feeling. He wished his mother were alive. He had been very close to her. Now his father had no one to look after him, only a son who didn't like him, and as if Mark needed to touch some personal things that would make his father seem less like a stranger, he searched through the closets of his bedroom. He touched the suits and jackets, and then, after hesitating, brooding and feeling like an intruder, he entered his mother's bedroom, untouched since the day she had died, everything left there as if they waited for her to walk in again. Her husband had made it a rule that nothing in this lovely room be disturbed, and he wouldn't go into the room himself, as if he believed she had some secret tender understanding and had always felt it when he was with her in her room. Mark began opening her bedroom closets and dresser drawers. He held up a little beaded bag, wrapped in tissue paper, which he had never seen before, and long white kid gloves. Then he turned to the old weathered pine chest, a family heirloom she had used as a girl as a hope chest. When he opened it there was a smell of camphor. Under the folded, faded white wedding dress, and in a chamois casing, he found a diary-journal, his father's, his time in Paris when he was twenty-six.

Sitting on his mother's pale-blue chaise longue, he began to read. In this journal, if not in real life, his father was a painter, a real painter, driven to paint in his own way and believing he was on to a new technique. He told about living in his little old hotel with the faded carpet on the stairs near the corner of Raspail and the boulevard du Montparnasse. He loved the life in The Quarter. He showed it in the way he recorded little scenes in the life around him. He told of the day he had sat at the Deux Magots a table away from the great Matisse just at nightfall when the last light was touching the old eleventh-century tower of St Germain des Prés across the square, the ancient tower, all white in the last flash of sunlight. On another day he met Derain and on the same day he saw André Gide coming across the square with Jean Cocteau. Then there were drawings of women. Little sketches, grotesques, a little like George Grosz. At that time of much experimental painting, he believed he could find a style, the brush working automatically, the brush directed by a rhythm, the style transforming the object. The seeing was in the way the brush took off from the start. The brush by itself, moving in its free rhythm, would transform objects. Maybe this was too theoretical, maybe too much of it was in his head, but it drove him on. He must have painted a hundred pictures before he ran out of money. At that time, he wrote in the journal that he would go home, save money and return to this little Paris hotel.

Of course he never returned to the hotel. At home he got a job in the creative department of the advertising agency. He got married. He learned the business. After fifteen years he became an owner. And Mark had never heard him talk about painting or Paris. Nor did he have any friends among the local painters; and as for the work he had done in Paris, he must have told himself it was worthless and had it destroyed. Sitting very still, pondering, Mark grew angry. He felt cheated of any knowledge of his father, cheated of the warmth and loving nature of a real father. Yes, cheated. A man with an interesting poetical urge a son would have loved had turned his back on his own distinction. Yet why had he wanted his wife to have the journal? He must have given it to her. Why? And she, knowing him as he had been, and knowing him as he had become, had kept the diary hidden as if it were evidence of a crime committed somewhere.

Shaken, Mark hurried out to visit his father's room in the hospital where he lay apparently asleep. For hours he sat beside him. From then on he went every day to that hospital room. His father's right side was paralyzed; he had lost his speech. His right hand and bare arm lay lifeless on the bed. The nurse coming into the room smiled when she saw him massaging the arm. His father's eyes, though, were alive; they would move from the door to the window, then to Mark's face, the expression changing a little as if he really recognized his son. Believing that he could be heard, Mark said he had found the journal. Bending over him, he talked quietly about how wonderful it would have been to know that young man in the journal. If his father could recover from the stroke they could visit Paris, he said, and sit in the cafés together. When there was only a long silence his heart sank. He wasn't even sure his father had recognized him. Glancing at his balding head on the white pillow, the eyes closed now, he wondered how his father had been able to turn his back so completely on the passion of his youth, even become someone else.

Late in the afternoon of that last day in the hospital, after a little sleep, his father's eyes opened. A look of recognition was in the pale blue eyes; the lips tried to form words, failed, tried again, then the left hand, the good one, came out and gripped Mark's hand, squeezing it hard three times as the eyes pleaded desperately. But pleaded for what? Confused, shaking his head helplessly, Mark blurted out, "It's all right, Dad. When you get a little better and get out of here, we'll take a trip. We'll go to Paris together. You and me. How about it?" Later that night his father had another stroke and died.

When Mark told Harold Hines at his father's funeral that the lawyers handling his father's estate were advancing him a little money and he was going to Paris for a week or two, Hines approved. "I like a young fellow to get out of the country and look around. You'll be a better journalist. It'll help shake the dust of graduate school out of your brain. If you think you see a story in Paris write it, send it. I'd like to see it." They buried Mark's father. And Mark, in the Paris hotel now, believed his father would like to be there with him. It made him feel good. He could go to bed feeling good. But it was only ten-thirty and he wanted something to read in bed.

He was alone in the elevator going down. When it stopped at the fourth floor, two middle-aged Americans entered, wearing beautiful expensive suits, with wide lapels, and both their faces shining with pink freshly shaven executive success, their grey hair slicked back. One of them, with a little grey moustache and the light-grey suit, held a carving under his arm, a naked and shining African black two feet long. After appraising Mark boldly, taking in his red jersey, brown slacks and hair that was a little too long and satisfied with his judgment of what he saw, this American thrust out the African carving. "Excuse me," he said, "would you know anything about these things?"

"What is it?"

"An original African carving. See?" And he held it up higher.

"Well, but where did you get it?"

"Right outside at the hotel entrance. A Moroccan sitting out there on the pavement has these things."

"Well, what do you want to know?"

"What do you think it's worth?"

"What's he asking?"

"A hundred and fifty dollars. Is it any good? I just showed it to my wife. She's not sure. What do you think?"

The faces of the earnest, well-groomed, well-off men told Mark that they recognized that he was not like them. He had a certain casual air. But he was surprised and flattered. As for the piece, he had seen something like it a hundred times. He liked collecting things himself. This piece could have been turned out in a factory. But this man could certainly afford the piece and what did it matter that the Moroccan, squatting on the pavement at the door, was robbing him? Then Mark felt torn; the grey-moustached rich man had appealed to him with such a candour.

"Well, that piece," he said, "is not worth a hundred and fifty dollars. In fact I've seen it myself in a newpaperman's office. Nice though, isn't it?"

"What's it worth then — if anything?"

"Oh, I don't know. Let's see. Fifty-five. Take it home but not for your house. Use it as a decoration in your office. It'll look great there."

"Thanks," said the man with respect. That was all.

When the elevator stopped, they all got out; the two Americans stood talking, and Mark, full of curiosity, sauntered out to the street. Twenty feet to the left of the entrance he saw the Moroccan, sitting cross-legged on a little mat. Beside him were other small carvings and pieces of jewellery. Lights from passing cars lit up the brown young face of the Moroccan who, with a big grin, accosted pas- sersby, pointing to his wares. Moving twenty feet away from the entrance, Mark waited. Soon the executive, who held the carving, came out and thrust it at the Moroccan as if reject- ing it. The Moroccan, suddenly on his feet, gestured violently. He grabbed the American's arm. They haggled. Finally, the American took out his wallet, offered some bills, then shrugging, began to put the bills back in the wallet.

Grabbing his arm again the Moroccan took the proffered bills. Back in the light of the hotel entrance the two well-off Americans, now smiling at each other, looked like very satis- fied competent businessmen. Squatting on his little rug the Moroccan had his big happy grin again. It was all very satis- factory even to Mark; he had solved a small moral dilemma. He had been honest with the affluent American who knew nothing of art but knew how to bargain, and yet he had made sure he helped the Moroccan make his sale. It was gratifying, too, that the businessmen, scrutinizing him shrewdly, had seen he was not of their world. As he was about to re-enter the hotel a car stopped and an American of fifty got out. A young woman leaned out of the car and kis- sed him warmly. Within two minutes two other cars, two Mercedes, brought Americans to the hotel; there was the same warm kiss at the car window, the cheerful goodbye and the smiling and satisfied Americans entered the hotel. Pros- titutes in expensive small cars — it would not have been like this in his father's time, Mark thought as he went in and got *Le Monde* at the newsstand. Back in his room he undressed and then, in bed, thumbing through the pages he sat up, startled. A picture of Jeremy Monk! A feature story about the French edition of a Monk book, and Monk was a cause of scandal among his left-wing friends and Marxists. As the critic wrote, Monk, the secret conscience to British socialists, who had been invited to Moscow by the Russian writers union wanting to honour him as the incorruptible supporter of the great Russian people, had let them all down. Even Sartre felt let down. Didn't Sartre really know him? Didn't de Beauvoir, either? Mark thought scornfully. Touring Leningrad with a woman interpreter — since he had no Russian himself — Monk had had little human conversations with anyone he met along the way, engineers, bus drivers, dancers, prostitutes in hotels, Kremlin men . . . just trying to get the hang of the way these citizens saw themselves in their daily lives . . . apparently innocent little human conversations that didn't bother the interpreter. All this would have been fine. The conclusion, though, that wounded Monk's French friends, delighted Mark. He smiled to himself; he read it and re-read it; it was quoted by the critic. In each man, Monk had written, was a secret domain. Every man or woman was sovereign of this domain and though a man sometimes might have to remain silent to protect his sovereignty, or appear to acquiesce, somehow he had to preserve that faint secret unconquerable area of self-respect. He could never surrender this secret domain or permit an alien occupation. Oh, there were some, the fierce secret silent ones who never gave in — but what distressed Monk was that he had found so many young intellectuals who had forgotten that a man had ever had a secret domain. This was even worse than a surrender. Putting down the paper Mark thought, all just like Monk, just like Monk! And feeling good, he turned out the light and soon fell asleep and dreamt of a thousand freshly laundered American executives in expensive suits lining up to consult him about African art.

◊ TWO ◊

AT NOONTIME HE TOOK A taxi to the corner of the boulevard du Montparnasse and the boulevard Raspail. The cafés were there on the corner just as they had been in his father's time, the Rotonde across the street from the Dôme, the Dôme terrace now just half the size he had expected, a movie theatre between the Dôme and La Coupole. Across from La Coupole was Le Sélect, his father's all-night café. Everything was in position but the hotel. He couldn't find the hotel. Walking down Raspail for a block, he cut back to rue Montparnasse, then back to the boulevard, to La Coupole to have a beer and talk to a waiter who told him there was an old hotel on a little side street almost opposite La Coupole. In five minutes he had found this hotel. He had been fooled by the smart new entrance. The small lobby, however, had carpeting as did the stairs. The middle-aged man at the desk who had long slicked-back black hair and tired eyes, said a room was available on the second floor. It was an old room, small, clean and dark, not a room where a painter could have worked. In the neighbourhood, however, he told himself, there could have been an atelier belonging to another painter which his father could have used. Coming down the stairs he paused, listening, waiting for an inner voice to tell him this was the right place. Though he heard no voice he knew he should take the room and he got a taxi, crossed the river, checked out of the Hilton Continental and having settled in the new place, he sat at Le Sélect, watching street people, imagining some of the faces in the crowd that might have passed forty years ago.

For the next two days he wandered around Montparnasse, finding the right places. In a ten-minute walk along Montparnasse he found La Closerie des Lilas, but the café didn't look right to him. There were no longer tables under chestnut trees where, as his father had said, street musicians had played. And no chestnut trees. Just a small terrace fenced in like a chicken coop. Inside, and beside the cash register, was a drawing of Hemingway, and on the mahogany-coloured tables many little brass plaques with the names of writers who had been patrons. Next day, going far down the boulevard St Germain, he found the Deux Magots, but because the terrace was crowded with Americans, he could not believe it was the same café where his father had sat with Derain. Yet it was; the old church tower was there in the sunlight across the square, and as of old, a mime on the pavement with his little table was doing magic tricks and passing the hat. But whether he was wandering around discovering little courtyards and art shops and cemeteries, or sitting in the Luxembourg Garden watching the children sail little boats on the pond, Mark never once felt lonely or in need of company.

On the third night, for the first time, he wore his black fedora. At home he would never have worn it, but here in The Quarter it amused him to think it would look right worn with the brim turned down all around. Looking at himself in the mirror he regretted that he did not have a beard. On his way to dinner at La Coupole, encountering a flower girl, he bought three gardenias which he carried carefully until, sitting at his table, he asked his convivial waiter to bring him an extra glass of water for his flowers. After dinner, when he moved out to the terrace, he took the glass with him, placing it beside his drink, and sat there contentedly.

Across the street the crowded terrace of Le Sélect was a blaze of light, as was La Rotonde, and on this side, the Dôme, the whole corner a big bowl of light hanging there in the night as it must have hung there forty years before.

As he stared happily at this bowl of golden light he fell into a trance, an expectant smile on his face, and he watched figures held so long in his imagination — the living and the dead — coming out of side-street shadows into the brightness; isolated, lonely figures, some coming from the boul' Mich, some from far down St Germain and from little streets and cellars by the river, the shadows hiding their isolation, their anguish, the death in them, till one by one coming into the bowl of light they came together in a little parade. But now they all had faces, the living and the dead in the bright gold dome there on the corner; Appolinaire, and Oscar Wilde waiting with the young André Gide, and Cocteau, holding up his beautiful hands, and Modigliani, staggering, but young, very young, and Fujita, the Japanese with his bangs, then just a glimpse of the massive Matisse. And there — Joyce, after dining at the Trianon, and Hemingway wearing three heavy sweaters, then McAlmon, combing his hair, and the dapper Fitzgerald, now bright and sober, and Kiki, the lovely clowning Kiki. And Bubu of Montparnasse. Why not Bubu? He lives, too, still lives. All forever young in that bowl of light.

He came out of his trance only when an auburn-haired long-legged girl accompanied by a middle-aged man with a little black moustache sat down at the table just to the right of him. The girl was so beautiful Mark's face lit up, as if he had been waiting for her all day long, and lifting the gardenias from the glass he approached her. But it was to the man he spoke. Bowing respectfully he said, "Sir, excuse me but I had promised myself I would offer these gardenias to the first beautiful girl I saw tonight. Please give them to the lady." The abashed man, after hesitating, said something to the girl in a language Mark didn't understand, then smiling, handed her the flowers. Bowing her head gravely, the girl brushed the flowers under her nose, then, smiling at Mark, kissed the flowers.

As Mark returned to his table a man of sixty with a plume of white hair who was in a group two tables to the left, beamed his appreciation at Mark. This man's two companions, two solid well-dressed Frenchmen, got up, shook hands with the elderly man, and as they left him, Mark was aware that the man who had smiled in appreciation was Jeremy Monk. He looked just like his picture. Half standing, Mark stared, he couldn't help staring; the man had been in his life too long. All through college he had sat in the Hart House Library, missing lectures to read Monk on politics and literature; then, standing at the window, had watched figures hurrying across the campus and dreamt of Monk, coming to America, coming to Toronto, though he knew Monk never went on tours or made these personal appearances that help sell a book and make a man a big public personality. Monk just lived for the truth that was in his work. And there Monk was now, just two tables away, smiling at him. The puckish grin gave Monk's face a sudden ageless vitality. Nothing had been said. Nothing had happened. But something seemed to have happened. As Monk's smile vanished and he half turned away, the tightly drawn skin on his high-cheekboned face made the head look like a skull. Approaching nervously Mark said, "You're Jeremy Monk."

"That's right," he said.

"You smiled — "

"Yes. I liked your gesture, so did the lady."

"Well, it felt right."

"There in your black hat," Monk said, smiling. "Ah, there in your chair on the boulevard where you have so often wanted to be. Ah, yes. I remember. Right here at La Coupole."

"This is your café?"

"When I first came here. Yes."

"Around forty years ago?"

"Around that time, yes. Why?"

"My father was here then, Mr. Monk. He knew La Coupole, he used to sit here. He was a painter."

"What was his name?"

"Andrew Didion. My name's Mark Didion."

"Andrew Didion, a painter. No. But at your age when I was here I didn't know anybody. I was too shy. I wanted to write, but I was a nobody. I had heard that Ernest Hemingway was looking for someone to box with. I liked boxing, but I was far too shy to approach him."

"But you got to know them all, didn't you?"

"Well, time passes. Are you a painter?"

"No, Mr. Monk. I want to be a journalist."

"Not a painter, eh? Is your father still painting?"

"My father died just a month ago."

"Oh, I'm sorry. Well, at least you have his work. Do you like it?"

"I can't say. You see, I haven't seen any of his work."

"What? Come on now Mark Didion, surely that's a little strange. Weren't you interested? The reporter — the journalist in you?"

"The truth is, Mr. Monk, I didn't know he was a painter."

"Really?"

"Really."

"Your own father?" and he frowned. "Who told you then that he was a painter? Come on. Sit down. Have a drink with me," and he called the waiter. "The paintings are somewhere, aren't they?" he asked. "Or is that why you're here?" and his warm beguiling smile made Mark feel that it was important to Monk to know about his father. He began to talk. At first he was shy, but the changing expression on Monk's face drew him out. Now it had the gravity of some deep human involvement; the steady blue eyes were so full of perception they invited Mark to go on, and he went on with the story till the waiter appearing at the table, interrupted him. Then fumbling awkwardly in his pocket for his cigarettes, he said, "This is absurd, Mr. Monk. This is wild. I'm here with you and I'm telling you all about me. I must be out of my head. There were days at college when I used to imagine a time might come when I could sit with you like this. . . ." His voice had changed a little, he now had a happy smile. "I wanted to tell you about a wonderful thing in your writing — for me, Mr. Monk, I mean. No matter the situation I'd see you there on the page — trying to tell the truth. It was important to me to have you there the way you often said — always on the side of the truth." With a boyish laugh he went on, "I guess I liked to think there was someone in the world who'd always be truly himself, maybe born just to be himself, no matter where his life took him." Then he stopped, embarrassed because the expression in Monk's eyes changed. "I guess I've been waiting to say this, Mr. Monk."

"You touch me, Mark," Monk said, taken aback. "Yes, you really touch me." At a loss for words, he fell silent. Then, clearing his throat, he said, "I know you're wondering if there's anyone left around here who might have known your father. Well, what are you doing tonight?"

"Just sitting here, I guess. I like sitting here."

"Why don't you come along with me. There's a party in an atelier over by the Observatoire. A painter named Jethroe. Ever hear of him? No? Well, he's been around here for forty years. Knew Matisse and Miró. And he's the one man I know who might remember your father." As they got up he took Mark's arm; he was two inches taller. He held Mark's arm firmly and easily as if he knew he was right in his sudden liking for him, and Mark in his turn, responding, tucked in his arm a little.

Arm in arm they walked slowly out of the blaze of light on the corner and along Montparnasse. Then they heard dance-hall music. Monk, stopping, pointed across the street. "That's the 'Jockey.' I remember when Hiler took it over. Your father would have known Hiler. Everybody knew Hiler."

And Mark said, "Talking about my father, Mr. Monk — there's a thing I couldn't figure out. In the hospital when his hand came out to me there were tears in his eyes, tears streaming down his cheeks. Why do you think that was, Mr. Monk?"

"Well, obviously he regretted something. Your relationship perhaps?"

"Something he thought he had done to me?"

"Maybe. More like something about himself. Perhaps some sin against himself."

"A strange remark coming from you, isn't it?"

"How so?"

"You don't sound like a Marxist now."

"My father was a clergyman, didn't you know?" and he chuckled.

Then Mark told him he was anxious to read the Russian book; it sounded fascinating. Yes, but would it be misunderstood, Monk said. He would see that Mark got a copy if he left his address with him, and as they walked in step Mark was filled with the wonder of being there at this hour, with the man who had shaped his thinking, talking with him on a street that was like a sacred path where all the dead ones he had dreamt about had walked. They had come to La Closerie des Lilas, the lights under the trees and it struck him that Monk and his own father, as young men, had sat under those trees.

"This is where we turn up," Monk said. "First, why don't you call me Jeremy? All right? The atelier is a few minutes away up there." Then, taking Mark's arm again, "You know why I like you, Mark?"

"I think you said I reminded you of yourself here at my age," Mark said.

"No. You didn't ask me what Joyce was really like."

"Really like? Do you know?"

"Nor what Hemingway was really like."

"I was more interested in you, Jeremy, and what you're really like."

"Oh, good, and when you find out you can let me know."

◊ T H R E E ◊

AS THEY TURNED UP THE
street Mark told him he
had been reading André Malraux's journal, and asked if he
had known Malraux in the days of the Spanish Civil War. Of
course he had known Malraux, he said. He had known him
well, an aviator and a hero and even then a great figure — as
big as Hemingway. "Ah, these great personalities," Mark
said. "The Republicans lacked the legions, but they had the
great personalities who seemed to think of it as their own
war." Nowadays he never heard from Malraux, Monk said,
but why should he? Malraux worked for de Gaulle now and
here in France he was bigger than ever — a man of great
memories. He was still talking about Malraux when they
turned into the courtyard and arrived at the Jethroe atelier.
The painter's young wife greeted them at the door; then
they moved into the atelier.

The atelier had a great window two storeys high facing
the courtyard. Mrs. Jethroe had long red-gold hair, a
lovely face with wild blue eyes and wore a low-cut black
dress, and after she had hugged Jeremy Monk she stepped
back, looked at him, opened her arms again, and after he
kissed her, her eyes remained on him even though she
held out her hand to Mark. "I'm a Hungarian, you see,"
she said, and maybe she was, but her English was perfect.
Behind her, smiling and waiting, was a tall, black-haired,
black-eyed girl whose nose had a gentle hook. The nose

fascinated Mark; it directed his eyes to her full red mouth and lips now parted expectantly as she waited her turn for Monk's affectionate loving embrace.

In the big atelier there were some fifteen guests: older women and middle-aged men, meeting and parting against the backdrop of the great window that had a strange lace-like shadow at least three feet deep at the top. Taking Mark's arm, Monk said, "It's Jethroe you want to meet. Come on. He's lying down resting. He strained his back playing tennis. Though he's my age, no, a little older, he plays every day. He's quite mad." A narrow spiral stairway led to a railed balcony which was furnished like a small living room with a deep couch, a coffee table and bookshelves on the back wall. The sixty-five-year-old Jethroe, half bald, the baldness circled by a crown of grey hair, was stretched out on the couch. He had on an open-necked blue denim shirt. There was strength in his tanned, lean face but his blue eyes were soft and mild. You could see the cords and veins in his bare arms. He was all muscle. And there, having a drink with him, was a Frenchman, a man of fifty, who obviously had no warm feeling for Jeremy Monk, for after a cool greeting he left.

Motioning to Mark to sit beside him, Jethroe poured him a Scotch. "So your father was around here at the end of the twenties, you say. What was his name again?"

"Andrew Didion."

"Andrew Didion. A painter."

"And he used to sit at La Coupole."

"Andrew Didion. Hm. Hm. And how long was he around here?"

"Nearly two years, I think."

"Hm. Hm. No. I don't remember anyone by that name. Now look, it doesn't mean anything. I might have sat just a few tables away. Or right next to him. I might have talked to him. But how would I know? That was the way it was. If I saw a picture of him there's a chance I might say, that's the

fellow who used to sit every night at La Coupole. Did he
look like you?"

"At my age? I don't know." Mark said. "They say I look
like my mother. It's too bad, at first it didn't seem too much
to expect, but it was just a chance," and then realizing he
was not going to find anyone around here who had known
his father he grew satisfied — strangely satisfied. In his imagination he could see his father in these faces. He could see
him sitting near Monk at some neighbourhood café, and it
was satisfying to do so.

"Ah, the cafés," Jethroe said. "It's always, 'Who's that sitting at the next table?' Well, I've always been a great believer
in the cafés. Who's this coming?" They heard steps on the
stairs. "Who's this?" said Jethroe, on his feet now. He
looked downstairs. "Ah, Lapierre, a fine poet from Bordeaux. A Stalinist. When he was young, he was a friend of
Bernanos. We heard they quarrelled over Marxism." The
Stalinist poet and his young lover, a Syrian, now on the balcony, embraced Jethroe. The poet was barely five feet tall,
and, so it seemed, a yard wide. His head was like a soccer
ball planted on massive shoulders, a big bearded ball on
which he had stuck a beret. And the lover, tall, slender and
elegant and no more than twenty-five, had beautiful, sad,
wise eyes. The poet sat down with Jethroe. They talked in
French. The Syrian, after appraising Mark, decided to talk in
English. He had never been to Canada, he said. Was it so
very cold? He had been born in a village near ancient
Babylon. Archeology was his hobby. He was full of fascinating information about the Babylonian ruins, but Mark, listening with one ear to the French conversation, heard the
massive poet, the Stalinist, tell Jethroe that there was too
much respect for the so-called integrity of Jeremy Monk.
Monk could do a lot of harm to the whole socialist movement with his goddamned integrity. There had to be some
discipline and Jeremy simply could not take the discipline.

The poet did not sound like a poet. The beautiful young man from Babylon with his wise soft eyes ought to have been the poet, Mark thought.

Rubbing a hand over his skinny corded arm, Jethroe, shrugging, said, "Yes, Jeremy has a remarkable kind of mind. A most subtle way of thinking. In any other kind of man that mind could be very dangerous; it's so persuasive. But in Jeremy it's all right. He happens to be a good man. I don't know what he's up to now. Anyway, I think his influence is largely personal. People can feel he's a good man." Jethroe's comment upset Mark. Meeting Mark's hostile eyes the poet, frowning, stood up, and the Babylonian hopped up, too. In the parting, the massive poet, his arms now around Jethroe, ignored Mark. Even while going downstairs he talked only to Jethroe, calling up to him. Left alone for the moment, Mark stood at the balcony rail looking down on the guests who stood in little groups that kept breaking up, except for the one group, the largest one — those who had gathered around Jeremy Monk. There he was with his white hair fluffed out a little, a white bonnet on his young-old face, the head like a skull, a gaping mouth opening and closing. He wasn't handsome; he wasn't ugly, yet there was something magnetically compelling in the face that changed so quickly from a noble gravity to the congenial available smile and Mark, watching, felt a little surge of confidence in himself and his right to be there.

A woman of forty in black slacks and a blue and silver top who moved quickly from one group to another listening intently, then gliding away, caught his eye. Auburn haired and high checkboned, she had markedly square shoulders and she obviously had had too much to drink. "She darts around like a bird," he said as Jethroe, joining him at the rail, handed him a drink.

"That's Rebecca," Jethroe said.

"Who's Rebecca?"

"We all look after Rebecca."

"I see, and that strange jagged shadow I see at the top of the window — it fascinates me."

"It's not a shadow," Jethroe said.

"No? What is it?"

"Dirt."

"Dirt?"

"Years and years of dirt. You see the window cleaner didn't come. I think he died. I left it. Looks interesting, doesn't it?"

"It looks like an etching," Mark said, as he watched Jethroe's wife approaching Jeremy Monk, who waited, both hands held out to her. The warm affection in her wild lovely face stirred Mark; he felt a little ache of longing for her. Yet she was the wife of this elderly man beside him.

"Yes," Jethroe said calmly, as if he knew exactly what Mark was thinking, "she has her own lovers, you know."

"Of course, of course," Mark said casually, hiding the shock he felt from Jethroe's candour and implying he understood her relationship with many lovers was a trivial thing for Jethroe. But what was her need for Jethroe, he wondered, the need he satisfied? "Your friend, the poet," he said, changing the subject quickly. "I don't know his work. You say he's good?"

"Very good. You should read him."

"Why is nature so unfair? The poet looks like a big dwarf wrestler. On the other hand, his lover . . ."

"The lover has no talent."

"Just nature's approval, Mr. Jethroe."

"Which would you rather have? A beautiful face, nature's approval, or some real talent?"

"I'd take the talent, I think."

"Who wouldn't? Ah, look at our friend Jeremy. Just watch him. Watch our friends gradually being pulled toward him, as if they know he'll make things more interesting."

"And the handsome woman going slowly toward him."

"Gabrielle Latouche. Surely you know her work. All the young women of the world love her, and a friend of Sartre's to boot. You can't beat that, can you? And yet I have always thought she wears porcelain pants. Oh, don't take my word for it. You'd have to talk to Jeremy. Well, my back feels rested. Let's go down." He led the way slowly down the narrow winding stairs.

At the long table where the stately Madame Latouche and Jeremy Monk sat opposite each other, Mark, feeling he was making himself conspicuous, standing behind Monk, moved away from the table. A man of thirty, at loose ends himself, said to him, "My name is Heffernan." He had an English accent. "I hear you're from Canada." So they all knew he was Jeremy's friend. Heffernan said he had been in Paris since the spring. He was writing a book about Jeremy whom he had first met at Oxford where Jeremy had given one lecture. "I don't know how he'll take all this fuss about him and his book. There's a big fuss about it in London, too, you know," and he kept smiling and smiling and on him was the sweet smell of marijuana.

At first Heffernan talked with that half-apologetic air the English use when they try, quickly as they listen, to get the hang of you, to know by your accent what school you went to and what you father did for a living. Being a Canadian, Mark couldn't be placed, and one had to be cautious. If he got this book on Jeremy finished, Heffernan said, he would try and sell a piece of it to the *New Yorker*. Like so many young Englishmen he wanted to write in the *New Yorker*. While they talked the square-shouldered Rebecca, weaving a little, glided by on her way to the washroom. Up close she had a fixed, sullen expression, her eyes puffy as if she had been crying and was hurrying to a place where she might cry again. "Excuse me, Heffernan," Mark said. "Who is this Rebecca?"

"An Australian. A painter."

"She looks as if she's been crying."

"No doubt about it, old boy."

"Doesn't anyone care?"

"We let her be, Didion. Let her be. Very gently, Didion, we all just let her be."

"What's the matter with her?"

"Why Jeremy Monk's the matter with her, poor soul. She lived with him for over a year in an apartment over by the Santé prison. Now he's left her. She's still in the apartment and he's moved to the Lutétia hotel where he'll be till he goes back to London. While he's here, she'll keep coming to these parties and drinking herself silly with no one apparently noticing. Then, and this is lovely — just before she gets blotto Jethroe asks someone to take her home."

"Doesn't leave the poor woman with much dignity, does it?" Mark said.

"Dignity?"

"Yeah. Why not take her home before she makes a spectacle of herself?"

"Dignity! I don't know, Didion. Just letting her be, then looking after her — ah, that's real compassion, that's real dignity, isn't it, old boy?" Smiling his half-beatific, half-silly smile, he moved toward the group at the table and standing behind Monk, put his hand on his shoulder. Without turning, still talking, Monk removed the hand. Off by himself, his eyes on the washroom door, Mark imagined that if he could talk to the Australian painter she might tell him little secrets, things about Monk, things Monk might never write about himself, and give him surprising glimpses into Monk's private world. No one had really done this. Even that brilliant wild radical Italian journalist who called herself simply Renata, and who could get surprising interviews with all the great European strongmen, had failed to do this in her memoir of her months with Monk on one of the Greek islands. She had told about her delight in his touch, how she had felt in him a mysterious adoration of her flesh, the magic in their partings and meetings and partings, but had known nothing about the secret of his need for a new woman, always a new woman. But to this day Renata's blessing was on him and would remain on him no matter who his new woman was. The Australian woman, who had come from the washroom, was now close by. Mark went to speak to her, then grew afraid that if the others saw him they would turn up their noses at him for not doing as they did — let the woman just be — accept her right to be there with her resentful, anguished heart. Then the sound of soft music came from the dimly lit far end of the atelier and high on the great studio window was a glint of moonlight coming through the great lacy dirt shadow, and near the base of the window, a slender girl all by herself examined one of the Jethroe canvases stacked against the wall.

Approaching her, waiting for her to turn and wondering why she wouldn't, he asked finally, "Do you like it?"

"I don't know, and may never know," she said calmly, without turning away from the painting.

"It troubles you?"

"Not at all. It's just there. It's outside me. And you?" She turned, facing him. About twenty-four, dark haired and brown eyed, she eyed him calmly. At first he thought she wasn't really pretty, and then at a second glance she seemed to him a striking beauty of another time. He seemed to see medieval stained-glass windows behind her. "Well," he stammered. "Well," wondering if he had had too much to drink. "I don't know how to look at it. I'm not a painter."

"Nobody is going to tell you how to look at it," she said.

"Are you a painter?"

"Well, sometimes I think so."

"Realistic? A realistic painter?"

"Real? When is it real? I don't know. I mean sometimes I know. Yes, sometimes I seem to catch a glimpse of something real, never seen before. I mean like Monet's garden pictures," and then she grinned; it was not a smile, the gravity of her calm mysteriously ancient young face was shattered by a wide grin that made him catch his breath, and he heard soft music, a street singer humming softly. Saying nothing he slipped his arm around her waist, dancing with her in a little circle, feeling her in easy step with him. Then, he couldn't help himself; he kissed her on the mouth. She had a smoky breath.

Stepping back, her face full of the untroubled calmness, she waited.

"Who are you?" he asked.

"Cretia Sampari."

"You live here, Cretia?"

"My home is Rome. And you're Jeremy's friend, aren't you?" she asked. Taking his hand she said, "You really should see the Monet garden pictures." Then, leaving him, she called back, "I'll show them to you," and as he watched the free swing of her legs and the line of her shoulders, all in a loose easy confident motion, he seemed to be still feeling the intimate pressure of her fingers on his hand, the feel of her waist in his arm, the taste of her smoky breath, all having an effect on him that was utterly unfamiliar: a heightened awareness of the disparate colours of the women's dresses, the warmth of hanging rugs on the walls, Mrs. Jethroe's redgold hair, the Greek girl's fascinating nose, everything in a fresh warm soft brightness that delighted his senses. Approaching the still blissfully smiling Heffernan he asked, "Who's that girl?"

"Her?" he answered. "Oh, Cretia. Yes, she paints. At least I think she does. At least she's been studying here; she gets around a lot. An Italian. Lives out at the Bois de Boulogne. Goes riding a lot. Hold on a moment. I remember now. Her mother, an Irishwoman, very successful as an actress here in France, married a rich Italian. And yes, let me see. Yes, she has a bishop for an uncle too. And she went to school in England. How's that?"

"You amaze me," Mark said, lifting his glass to the Englishman.

Apparently she was not aware that he stood beside her as they all listened intently to a clash of opinions among those at the table; the squat moon-faced Bordeaux poet, Sartre's friend, Michelle, and Jeremy Monk. They were talking about Monk's book. The poet stubbornly maintained that it should not have been written. The socialist state, as it was in Russia, was like a pottery bowl, and the book, finding a hairline crack in the bowl, offered an invitation to others to widen the crack. Then what? A broken bowl. Oh, yes, he said, the book would get a lot of attention for all the wrong reasons. But every good Marxist in France was disappointed in Jeremy Monk.

"A good Marxist. Oh, yes," Monk said with his gentle smile. His expression of profound sympathetic concern as he listened made every word said against him seem movingly important. "But, you see, my friend, what's a good Marxist? The plain truth is there are no good Marxists in France. Even if France went communist tomorrow they still wouldn't be good Marxists. They can't be. They're French. You know that's true, Michelle."

"There's some truth in it," said the friend of Sartre smiling. For one so imposing, so handsome, it was almost an amusingly mischievous smile. Indeed, on a lesser woman it might have been a wink, implying she and Jeremy Monk shared some secret. "The mistake here is in thinking that Marx was a philosopher," she said. "He was an economist. It's others who try to make him into a philosopher who teaches us how to live, and how foolish that is."

"Spoken like a Frenchwoman," Monk said. As his eyes met hers in another moment of mysterious intimacy, the whole expression on her face changed. There was now a new shy warmth in her face, and Mark wondered if he really saw this sensual warmth in Michelle, or was it coming to him from Cretia as he brushed against her.

He had never liked Michelle's work or her vast influence. She was a chatterbox. In her centre of Paris intellection, she could take a trivial event like a Sunday afternoon picnic in the country, worth at most a paragraph, and turn it into three pages of useless meditation about sexual matters and women's rights. Mark had concluded that she had little or no actual sexual experience, just fantasies. Yet now, watching her face, he was aware of her impulsive reaching to Monk for intimacy. No, a satisfaction of that intimacy, all in her eyes and shy smile. Or was it in all these smiling women? Or was it in his own head? No, it was like a flash of certainty that this imposing woman had slept with Jeremy Monk who knew the deep secret things about her; with her eyes she was making him remember. The other women, their eyes on Monk, were smiling too in a knowing sharing of some memory that quickened them. Jethroe's golden-haired Hungarian with her restless eyes, and the Greek woman with her fascinating nose also waited in a kind of warm smiling contentment for more of Monk's words. Mark believed then that Jeremy Monk had slept with them. And the Australian woman! Her too! How did he do it? What was it he knew about these women, or what did they know about him?

"Where's Jeff?" Mrs. Jethroe said suddenly. "Where's my husband?"

"Lying down for a few minutes," the poet said.

"He may have fallen asleep," she said. "I'll get him some coffee," and she went into her small kitchen.

A little later she returned bearing plates of cold cuts and then salad bowls and more cold cuts and cheeses. Her competence was astonishing, Mark thought. Then, looking around for Cretia, he wondered why she had moved away from him. Why wouldn't she look at him? The Greek and a

German girl, a photographer, who had travelled alone in the Middle East, and Mrs. Jethroe, whispering together, were making some plan that apparently did not include Cretia, who at first had joined them, then wandered away without a glance at Mark. The three women vanished. For the first time, Mark and Jeremy Monk were alone together. Monk's hand came out to Mark's arm, the pressure so friendly it made Mark feel good. It had been in his mind, Monk said, that Mark had told him he wanted to be a journalist and had a connection with a Toronto paper. Well, why shouldn't he do a story about the reception the Russian book was getting in Paris and London, and include an interview with him? He, indeed, might help Mark with the article. "That would be wonderful," Mark said. "Look, it's a deal. I'll rent a typewriter tomorrow."

"Do the article, Mark, and I'll have a go at it with you. It might be the right thing for you. I know you'll do a good job."

"How do you know?" Mark said. He couldn't figure out why Monk was so sure of him, for as far as he knew, he hadn't made one intelligent remark to him about anything. Yet Monk said, "You're very intelligent. That much I do know." Then Mark, looking up, saw Cretia coming toward them, smiling for the first time as she sat down. In the morning, Monk said, he would have the book sent to Mark's hotel. Those who were near the table left them alone since they were talking so earnestly. They kept talking till Jethroe's wife and her two friends, looking very pleased with themselves and giggling, returned. Getting up, Mark asked the German girl, who was now standing beside him, where had they been? The pretty photographer said that the Greek had told her and Jethroe's wife that a man she had known five years ago, now living in the neighbourhood and just a few minutes away, had got in touch with her. Five years ago her virginity had been bothering her; it was a nuisance; and she had deliberately picked on this man to deflower her. After the event she hadn't seen him again. Tonight she had been curious to see him. The three of them had just visited him in his apartment and had a drink with him. He had begged her to resume their friendship and she had laughed. She hadn't the slightest interest in him now.

Out of the corner of his eye, while he talked to the photographer, Mark caught a glimpse of Monk and Cretia sitting together and in a flash imagined he could see the blue stained-glass window behind her, blue like the pictures he had seen of the window in the Chartres cathedral. Stiffening, he watched Monk's hand go to Cretia's neck, the fingers playing with her hair and, lifting the hair, he kissed her neck, kissed her lightly and lovingly on the neck, then, whispered to her, making her laugh and whisper to him. Straining to hear, Mark tried to tell himself Monk's hands would be touching any of these pretty women if they sat close to him; it was Monk's delight in women.

◊ F O U R ◊

ALL NEXT MORNING, HE sat at La Coupole with croissants and coffee, reading the new Monk book that had been delivered to the hotel. He made some notes. His waiter told him where he could find a shop that rented typewriters. At this shop he rented a portable, got paper and carbons too, then went back to the hotel, and finished reading the book. He could see why some of Monk's friends were upset by the book. In the interviews, each one of this strange collection of Russian citizens was given a dignity and autonomy, as if a garbage collector's view of his socialist world was just as important as any party chairman's. Strange things were said. Strange questions were asked by Monk. Confused himself, Mark tried to get Monk at the Lutétia Hotel. He left his name. He waited in the hotel room, and about five Monk did call him. Monk said, yes, come to the hotel lounge in half an hour. It was a short walk down to boulevard Raspail and rue de Babylone where he stopped to look at the handsome stone hotel, all yellow white and shining in the hot sunlight. The hotel looked too expensive for Monk who had never made any real money from his books. He was just a big name among intellectuals and college students.

The hotel had a big elegant lounge, and at the back, in sight of the bar which was off to the side, Monk waited.

He had on a brown corduroy jacket and plaid shirt open at the throat, and as Mark came in he rose with his sudden wonderfully warm smile.

"So good to see you Mark," he said. "You sounded on the phone as if you'd been reading all day. How long are you staying around?"

"About a week, I think."

"And I'll be gone in four days. Too bad. Too bad. Well, at least you're going to see Monet's garden pictures."

"Oh, am I really going to see them?"

"Aren't you going?"

"Who says I am?"

"Cretia says so."

"You think she meant it?"

"You don't know Cretia."

"No, I don't know Cretia," and then he hesitated, trying to remember. "Tell me something, Jeremy. Last night at the party, what was her dress . . . I mean what colour was it?"

"Dark blue, and lace a lighter blue. Why?"

"I can only remember her face."

"Maybe you don't notice what women are wearing."

"Oh yes, I do. Jethroe's wife wore a low-cut black dress. Very low cut."

"Right. Very low cut."

"And the Australian painter. Black slacks and a silver belt low on her hips."

"And Cretia? Just a face?"

"Odd, isn't it," Mark said, laughing awkwardly as he took out his notebook. "The reception your book got here, Jeremy; it was a bit venomous, wasn't it?"

Laughing indulgently Monk explained it was a bad period in Paris literature. It was as if he felt embarrassed at being forced to tell the truth about a city he loved. Not in years had Paris been so provincial, he said. When Sartre got interested in politics he issued a trumpet call: "Now is the time for engagement — involvement." When he got bored with politics, another trumpet call. "Now is the time for disengagement." Robbe-Grillet — you could get all his literary effects by using a scissors on a manuscript and then rejoining the pieces at random. The death of bourgeois narrative, they called it. Bourgeois narrative. Imagine! As for the fashionable little battlegrounds over such things as structuralism, post-modernism, they were lifeless games, games in their heads, which was probably why Freud, in Paris of all places, was bigger than ever. . . . Imagine! Freud! All the neurotic intellectuals of Paris, turned in on themselves as usual, still under the spell of the biggest neurotic of them all. Mark liked listening, liked his voice above all, liked being there with him, and yet, as he listened he wondered if the light-hearted air didn't reveal some trouble at his heart's core. But what could trouble a man like Monk? Changing the subject, he asked Monk about the Vietnam War, expecting to hear some withering comment about American imperialism. Instead, Monk remained gravely silent. It was an awkward moment. Finally, Monk said, "I know how you feel about it, Mark. Oh, it's all a bloody mess. Just right for these times. All lies. If only the Americans knew what they're fighting for — " As he broke off, his eyes held Mark's almost fiercely.

"Jeremy," Mark said, "I know there's nothing in all those jungles worth dying for."

"You die for the thing you live for, don't you, Mark?"

"Come on, Jeremy. That's rubbish. That's a joke on all soldiers choking in a ditch. Dying gets you nowhere."

"Nowhere? I wonder. . . ." Then he added with a gentle consoling smile, "About that we'll have to wait and see, won't we, Mark?" and he looked at his watch. "Good heavens," he said, "we've been here an hour and a half. Well, just make it a good report. I know you will, and remember this Mark, there's nothing better than great and truthful reporting. Any brash American newspaperman can do an opinion column, Mark. The basis of all great writing is simply reporting. That is Joyce in *Ulysses*, a Dublin day, a brilliant reporter. And Tolstoy? The greatest of all reporters. Yet, some idiots will say of a journalist — he's just a reporter. Ah, Mark, you should hope they say that about you."

On the way to the door, Monk told him that if he finished the piece in the next two days he should bring it to him on the morning of the third day — the day he was to leave — and he would go over it with him.

Feeling too keyed up to go right back to his own hotel, he wandered down to the Deux Magots and sat on the terrace having a beer, and now, just as his father had written in his journal forty years ago — a mime on the pavement was trying to get out of a glass box and then passing the hat. He had a sandwich on the terrace, took a taxi back to his hotel, and immediately started to write the piece, then jumped up and cursed; he felt Monk standing behind him looking over his shoulder, and couldn't start till he got rid of him. "Goddamn it. If I can't write about Monk I'll never, never write about anything," he cried. "Who knows his work better than I do? and what do I care if he's watching me?" Carried away, he finally began to write. He told how he had met Monk and what Monk had meant in his life. Monk was a man who had heard the cry for liberation that was in the hearts of all men, which was why he was so important to a whole generation. And moreover, he was unique among Englishmen; he had no class sense at all. He had a simple direct style. A style right for all classes. At three in the morning he quit. Then in bed, he couldn't sleep. At ten he got up, had his breakfast at La Coupole and came back to the room to go on working. By day's end he had written twenty-five hundred words, a piece far too long for Harold Hines, but not too long for a weekend feature. He went to bed and slept.

In the morning he called Monk, who said he could have two hours after lunch, then he would leave for the airport. At two-thirty, they were in the corner of the lounge again. "Well, let's see the piece," Monk said. "Don't worry. I know it'll be good."

Sipping his drink, Mark waited and watched, and waited for some altering of expression on Monk's face. The expression never changed as he put one page and then another on the table.

Then he asked, "Am I like that now, Mark?"

"Well, I only know you now."

"No one would believe it, Mark. You seem to have known me years ago, years and years ago."

"I feel that I did."

"And you know me now. I go on being what I am, and thanks be to God that I am what I am." His hand on Mark's shoulder, his voice softening, he said, "And I can see you'll always know that I'm on the right track."

"Then the piece is all right?" Mark said.

Bending over the table, a pencil in his hand, Monk began to go over the manuscript line by line. Moving his chair a little so he could see what Monk was doing, Mark watched him strike out one word, then another. The firm strokes hurt Mark; the repeated strokes became a real ache. He saw sentences being changed and gradually he became outraged. He grew pale. He thought Monk was serving himself and compromising him and not giving a damn whether or not he liked it. Reading a sentence to himself, Monk's lips would move. All the little flourishes Mark had regarded as a display of his own talent, even if just a decorative display, Monk cut out. Hardly looking up, Monk pushed one of the pages toward Mark who, at first, wouldn't look at it. When he did he saw the pared sentences now had a rhythm of their own as well as a freshness and to his astonishment saw that the meaning hadn't been changed at all. He felt embarrassed and bewildered. When he nodded, Monk paid no attention; he just frowned, still talking to himself, utterly absorbed in what he was doing and then Mark felt a little emotional catch in his throat. Just for a moment. But it became one of the most beautiful moments of his whole life! He knew he was learning more about writing here than he would learn in the rest of his life and knew he would treasure those edited pages, always have them somewhere close at hand. "It's not just what you put in . . . it's what you leave out." Then the wonder of being here like this with Monk overwhelmed him. He knew why Monk was so important to him, but couldn't figure out how he seemed to have become just as important to Monk.

"There you are, Mark my boy," Monk said, shuffling the pages together and handing them to Mark. "I knew you would do a good job. It just needed a little touching up; I can do this kind of thing because I know what editors look for. Type it up, my boy. Send it home. Well, time now to part." He walked Mark to the door and following outside he stood on the wide steps. "I'm off to England to flog my book, something I've never done before, and after England, well, the American publisher wants me to go to New York. If the book gets off to a good start I may even go on the road. A book tour, Mark. It's what they all do nowadays, I understand. Send me the piece when it comes out and your address. It will come out, you know," he said. "It's good. It's really me."

Standing on the top step beside the uniformed doorman he waved at Mark, who was out on the sidewalk. The sunlight was on Monk's crown of white hair. His face with the high cheekbones and sunken cheeks made so oddly attractive by his jovial warmth, shone with ageless vitality. "I'm an old man with white hair," he called, laughing. "And for the first time I'm going on the road. A wild old man on the road, Mark. I'll be seeing you somewhere on the road. What do you say?"

"I'll be waiting somewhere down the road," Mark said and stood for a moment, made mute with embarrassment by the pain he felt at the parting.

Taking a few steps away, he stopped, bemused again, and the doorman who was getting him a taxi said, "Excuse me, sir. I could see your wallet in your hip pocket. Better put it in another pocket." As Mark did so, the taxi came and took him to the hotel, and as soon as he lay on the bed he fell sound asleep.

◊ F I V E ◊

I N JUST A FEW DAYS HE would be leaving Paris and Montparnasse, and he tried to lengthen each day. On the first day, he retyped his edited manuscript and got it away. On the second day, he loafed around on the streets; he went into department stores, just storing up a feeling about Paris, and on the street he looked into the faces of strangers. He told himself no one in Paris could have the slightest interest in him or his plans, and that even if he stayed on month after month there still would be the vast Parisian indifference to the stranger, his ways, his ambitions and the clothes he wore. This indifference and the casual French rudeness he experienced in brief encounters would always rankle him. Though he loved being there, he couldn't figure out why he felt so exhilarated on the streets, or why it stirred him just to catch a glimpse of a boat on the river. Finally he thought he could figure it out. Here he could believe that wanting to be a great journalist was important! The wanting, the striving, the failing, the planning, the dreaming seemed to be more important than it ever could be at home, even though no one here might ever know his name. After all, he had met Monk here. Lord knows whom he might meet in this indifferent city. Who else was there? Next morning, just before lunch, when he was in his hotel room, Cretia Sampari telephoned. She would come to the hotel after lunch and pick him up and take him to see the Monets, she said.

Waiting at the entrance to the hotel, he watched a motor-cycle with a girl in a leather jacket and helmet come down the street and pull up at the entrance, the motor still running. "Come on, Mark, get on," Cretia cried, and he thought, "What is this? Did I get her wrong?"

"Hello, Cretia," he said.

"What's the matter? Didn't you expect to hear from me?"

"I didn't know."

"I said I'd go with you didn't I?"

"Just casually, yes."

"I'm never just casual," she said gravely.

"Tell me something," he said. "Do you know the cathedral at Chartres?"

"Of course I do. Why?"

"Are there astonishing blue stained-glass windows behind the main altar?"

"Yes, and they're very beautiful. You mean you've read about them?"

"I've seen pictures. But that's not it. I mean I'd like to see you there — against the windows."

"Me? A figure against the window? Well, that can be arranged too," she said, shrugging. "It's the Monets this afternoon though. Come on. Get on — and hang on tight."

When he got on the seat behind her, she took his hands, circling his arms around her waist. As yet, because of the helmet, he couldn't see her face, see it as he had at the party. He could brush his nose on the back of her neck; under the rim of the helmet there were little brown curls. As the bike surged, his nose dipped in the curls. He couldn't talk; he couldn't be heard above the sound of the engine, so he hung on, marvelling at her confidence, weaving in and out of traffic. He kept breathing on her neck, a regular slow breathing, then blowing on the little curls, and under the smell of the helmet, he had the scent of her neck. His lips brushed against her neck. They said nothing till they got to the Bois de Boulogne neighbourhood, when she shouted, "I live out this way," pointing to the left. At the Marmottan Museum she let him dismount and wait at the entrance till she parked, and as she came toward him with her swinging easy stride he so admired, she took off her helmet. "Ah now, Cretia. Now I can see your face," he said.

"My face?"

"Your face. Yet it doesn't go with your walk."

"Or my bike?"

"That's right. The funny thing is if I close my eyes now I can't see you on a bike."

"How about a donkey?" she said. "Come on."

In all the rooms in the museum there was an utter silence. If a visitor raised a voice, others in the room stared as if some perfect reverie induced by the contemplation of a Monet was being rudely broken. In this kind of silence, Mark seemed to know her better, feel her coming closer. She led him to the room where the large Monets hung, the Monet of the garden — the bushes, the pond, the trees. Sitting with her, looking with her, he was shocked by a picture's bold freshness, an exultant glory in something so real it stunned him, wrenched at him; he was afraid it would vanish if he took a deep breath.

Nothing was said. They sat in silence together till she turned and her eyes widened in surprise. He was staring at her with the same rapt attention she had seen in his face while looking at the pond. Bemused, finding some secret satisfaction in this, she smiled to herself. "Do you remember asking me if I wanted to be a realistic painter?" she whispered.

"And you said, 'Real, what's real?'"

"Yeah, I did. Well, that pond," she whispered. "Like that! Seen incredibly like that! That's real, Mark."

"But no one else ever saw it like that," he whispered.

"That's it. Seen for the first and the only time as no one could ever see it again. I think those who try to see it again make it ordinary. Like anything seen again and again becomes ordinary," she whispered, and then they fell into a long silence, apparently like any other visitors in contemplation of the masterpieces on the wall, but he was wondering if the jolt of surprise and delight he had got from the picture was like the intense quickening he had got at Jethroe's place when first she had turned her face to him, and could it ever come again, and how real was it anyway?

Leaving the museum she said, "There's a little café nearby. We could have a beer. But don't let me forget I'm going out to dinner tonight and mustn't be late."

The little café had only three tables on the sidewalk. At one of the tables an old man kept pounding his cane on the pavement. He was blind. The café madame was gentle with him. "Jeremy Monk is a very good friend of yours, isn't he?" Mark asked.

"Oh yes. Dear Jeremy."

"He seems to have great affection for you."

"I'm sure of it. And I count on it."

"Is he such an old friend?"

"I met him about a year ago," she said. "It was in Rome. It was a big tribute to Renata, the Italian journalist, the beauty, or at least she once was a beauty. Afterwards some of us went to the Café de Paris on the Via Veneto. Do you know it? And there I talked to Jeremy. As a matter of fact it was Jeremy who advised me to come here to study."

"This Renata," he said. "I've seen those striking pictures of her. How old would you say she is?"

"About forty now, they say. I'd say she was older."

"About right for Jeremy, though; I'd guess he's over sixty, wouldn't you?"

"I don't know. I've never wondered how old he is."

"Maybe you should never ask. Maybe he's ageless."

"Anyway, a European woman doesn't care how old a man is if he interests her. And what woman wouldn't be interested in Jeremy? It's something in his nature, I think. He gives off something — women feel it — a giving — something they hardly knew they needed. Anyway, he's wiser than anyone I ever met."

"You mean about women?"

"Not just women. I mean he knows things." Smiling to herself, she said, "He's never tried to tell me anything about myself. 'No point to it,' he said. I am just as I should be and that's great." Drawing back, regarding him carefully, she asked, "Are you married, Mark?"

"No, I'm not."

"I didn't think you were."

"Does it show?"

"Something in your blue eyes tells me . . . oh, tells me what? I don't know . . ."

"That I nearly did get married," he said, and he told her about Elena, the girl he had been engaged to, a very pretty Jewish girl taking her Ph.D. in economics. But her father had come into it. Her father got sadder and sadder, day by day, and soon the sadness turned to sickness. He was orthodox, you see, and disappointed that Elena was to marry outside his tribe. So he stopped eating and was on the verge of a nervous breakdown. It was all too much. Tired of hearing about her melancholy father, and outraged, he shouted that he would not be discriminated against in this fashion. There were a lot of tearful insults and he walked out, which made the father very happy. Elena went back to her psychoanalyst with whom she spent too much time anyway.

"That's a story with a twist," Cretia said, getting up. "I should try and remember it. Yet, it was a stepping stone."

"To what?"

"To you being here with me at this little café, no? Well, come on," and leading the way back to the motorcycle she pulled on her helmet and he got on the seat behind her. Again his arms were around her waist but now his touch was different. She settled into his arms. Once she moved his hand a little, under her breast, and his body tingled. The curls at the back of her neck became just a tuft to tickle his lips and fill him with a strange sense of expectancy, and the bike swayed, rocking him as he cradled her. She had to know she was doing it. Yet when they reached his hotel she didn't even get off the motorcycle. With the engine still running, gripping the handle bars, she said, "In the morning you go, Mark?"

"In the morning I go."

"You're not an actor, Mark. You actually mean what you say. It must get you into a lot of trouble."

"Off and on," he said. "Take the helmet off." Then he kissed her, not on both cheeks, but on the mouth, on her parted lips, and her breath had the taste he remembered.

"You'll be back," she said.

"I don't know, Cretia. I don't know."

"I do. Don't you remember? We're to go to Chartres."

"The blue window at Chartres. That's right, Cretia," he called as she raced the engine. Then she vanished around the corner of the boulevard du Montparnasse. His thoughts in a whirl, he entered the hotel, and he remembered how he had first climbed these hotel stairs, believing his father had often done so forty years ago, but that day — the first day on the stairs — he had had no secret intimations, no hunches that he had come to the right room. Yet now this didn't matter. He could leave Montparnasse, believing he had been close to the only part of his father's life he wanted to know. Packing his bag he took his time. He walked up to La Coupole, and sat at the table of his favourite waiter who was always just a little bit drunk. After a Scotch and soda, he went out and looked around. He wished it had been dark; he wished the corner could be there again in a blaze of light, his bowl of light, and soon he was in the taxi on the way to the airport.

In the plane, with Paris far behind, the tall blonde stewardess came down the aisle with the magazines and newspapers. Taking the latest *London Observer*, he opened it at the book section to see if there was anything about Monk. Indeed there was. A whole page was given to Monk. The writer of the piece, a socialist himself, was harsher on Monk than any Paris critic had been. Doomsday Monk, he called him. Was the death in Monk's world, or in him? he asked. Jeremiah at the Wailing Wall — a man bored with his own past. Monk himself had written a short piece for the page. It was framed in the middle of the page with his picture. Monk wrote: "One morning, after a good night's sleep, I woke up refreshed, and lying in bed meditating, I became aware that I ought to be a contented man. I had got the world I had dreamt of when I was young. A time of a new sense of freedom. I don't mean that heady communal satisfaction I shared with so many watching the great freedom marches and parades for peace. No, this was something that had to do with how we all lived together. A wind had come out of the west, and on the wind a whisper, and the words whispered on this wind were, 'Let there be apathy for politics, all politicians are a bore, and let the rich get rich and the poor get poorer, it's going to happen anyway. Feel free at last about yourself. Let the uncorrupted noble savage within you come out and look around in the sunlight as he couldn't do in Rousseau's time, and drop all the buttoned-up coats, walk naked and unafraid, let the happy pop singers be your bards and prophets. Find your own style of living, your own style of coupling in which there are no bondages, just relationships. New relationships born of a new openness. Break down the language. Let there be no secret words that make a woman shiver. Let down your hair, let down your pants. Use your open heart and not your worn-out head, and enjoy, oh, do enjoy the divine relief in knowing there is no one moral authority, no one spiritual authority. Enjoy, too, the new frontiers of the imagination, the half-forgotten world of hallucination, the ancient world, so easily recovered with a few drugs.'

"This has been the whisper on the western wind, and the other day a middle-aged advertising executive said to me, 'I do my corporate job, but at night when I go home I take off my three-piece suit, and I'm happily a hippie and I feel so free.' A half-time freedom, to be sure. Even this advertising executive had heard the word on the western wind, and submitted . . . this strange general submission to what is now on the wind. No, this is not freedom or liberation. It's submission — the mysterious compulsion that drives lemmings over the cliff. A decade of young men and women all marching to the tune of the times and more in step with each other than when they all wore three-piece suits. They have no choice, so there's no freedom. What is this? I've written, I've fought for a political freedom for others. But this other, deeper personal freedom, the thing so mocked in these times, where do I go to find it?"

The old bastard. So that's what he really thinks of my generation? Mark thought. What in God's name has happened to him? He was so shaken he couldn't believe this was really Monk. As he closed his eyes, leaning back in the seat, feeling angry and betrayed, he tried to tell himself that Monk had simply got old and sour; the younger Monk would have loved these times as much as he did. The old man had let these wonderful years pass him by; he didn't even know what he had missed. Moved and stirred up, he thought of the years of his own growing, the years he loved, this happy decade, the sense of liberation, the search for new experiences, the songs they sang, the girls he had loved, the feeling that there was new energy all around him, and sitting up all night long talking with his friends about new free forms in music and painting. Oh, yes, the younger Monk would have known it was a wonderful time to be alive.

Calm now and grim, he lay back in the seat, then, as if in spite of himself, he thought of those words of Monk's: "This other deeper personal freedom . . . Where do I go to find it?" and he picked up the paper again, read those words and pondered. The words really sounded like Monk. Troubled and wondering, he thought, never mind the cockeyed, wrong-headed stuff about these times. What about this new freedom? The quest for freedom — it had always been his passion. Was it still his passion? "Where do I go to find it?" Strange words. What was he really up to? And the question kept coming back to him on the flight home.

I N THE GARDEN OF HIS OWN home, all in bright autumn sunlight, he poked away at the flowerbeds and wondered how the summer blooms could all wither and die in the short time he had been away. Then his neighbour, the seventy-year-old Mrs. Walton, born in the house she lived in, wearing her gardening gloves, a wicker basket on her arm, called, "I see you're home, Mark. How are you? Did you have a good trip?" Coming to the fence, she said, "By the way, yesterday I did something I haven't done for two years. I went downtown. I went to Eaton's. Do you ever go downtown?"

"I have to, Mrs. Walton."

"Yes, I suppose you do. But do you go on Yonge Street? It's awful what has happened to our Yonge Street. Men in yellow robes and shaven heads circling around in single file chanting in strange tongues. Young men loafing around with dirty long hair, all bums, Mark. Common prostitutes in doorways too. Yonge Street! I was glad to get home."

"The old town is gone, that's true," he said, then reflecting he went on. "Yet, do you know Mrs. Walton, coming in from the airport, coming along the lakefront, the city there in the distance, all the new office towers there like temples, new temples every six months. Of course we have no great monuments, no great tombs, but on the streets are all these new people, people from all over the world, Mrs. Walton.

The big new city. It's becoming, becoming — I don't know what — I kind of liked it, Mrs. Walton."

"Mark, I'm afraid you and I don't think alike," she said doubtfully.

"It's simply that the old town is gone, Mrs. Walton."

"Not around here it hasn't. This is still our neighbourhood."

"Yes, we're lucky," he said, humouring her. "We don't even have to cross our bridge over the ravine, do we, unless we want to."

"And thank god, we don't," she said. "I wouldn't walk across that bridge at night. Well, you grew up around here, Mark, and I know you won't forget it."

"I won't, Mrs. Walton."

"I'm glad to see you're home, Mark," and she left him.

It was the place where he had grown up, yes, but as soon as he had entered the house and was greeted by the Filipina housekeeper, he did not feel he had come home. For the first time since his father's death, he felt lonely in the big house where he had never had an intimate conversation with his father, a man who now seemed to be both young and old at the same time; when younger, so much closer to him; when older, so much more moving. Both gone, and Jeremy Monk apparently gone too, leaving a sour feeling. As he went into the house he thought, It's the autumn. Always the end of something. A lonely time. The leaves are starting to fall already. Maybe I should sell the place and go back to Paris. Did Cretia really believe we'd be going to Chartres? Who knows about these things? Then, on a hunch he telephoned Harold Hines, who by this time should have read his piece on Monk. Hines' secretary, after taking his name, said, "Please hold a minute," and then asked if he could be in Mr. Hines' office in half an hour.

Harold Hines, who never laughed out loud, and drank too much and had trouble with his wife, said, "Remember I told you you were cut out for journalism. Your father didn't think so. He was wrong. Well, there's your story," and he pointed to the newspaper spread out on his desk: last Saturday's entertainment section. "I knew about Monk years ago," Hines said. "I read his book on the Spanish Civil War when no one else did. He was never my man, but he's your man now. See. A full page, and a picture of your man." He was watching the changes that came on Mark's face as he read the page. "You're surprised, Mark? The space? Well, you got a break. Monk is news in London right now. It's all to the good for us. According to the London bureau, the young are throwing bricks at him, the socialists are writing him off as a renegade, the archbishop is praising him, and people who never heard of him now take cracks at him." Then turning to his secretary, he said, "Get Tom Mathers in here," and to Mark, "I want you to meet our city editor."

Mathers was a dark-eyed thin man who kept wetting his red lips. "So you're Mark Didion," he said. "I don't know what your experience is, but that's a very competent, very professional job. How in hell did you work the timing of the thing out so well with Monk? I'd like to give you an assignment sometime. Let's keep in touch. Good man, good work," and he shook hands.

When Mark left the office he had three copies of the edition that carried his story, but as soon as he got outside, he began to feel ill at ease. He owed this triumph to Monk. Monk had actually edited the story and touched it up, and remembering this became a humiliation. Yet he would have to send Monk a copy of the newspaper. He didn't want to have to write to Monk. Not now. He didn't want to hear from Monk.

He went into Phelan's Bar on lower Yonge and later moved uptown to Yorkville and Cowan's Bottom Line, but wherever he went he kept going over the words he would use writing to Monk. He ate in Cowan's. In his room at home he paced up and down scowling at his typewriter. Finally, he sat down and typed, "Dear Jeremy: Here's the story. I understand you're big in London now — the Russians and your wail about the world in the *Observer*." Then, for the sake of his own self-respect, he wrote, "What in hell has happened to you, Jeremy? Or do you even know?" Signing the letter, he clipped it to the newspaper page, put it in an envelope and hurried out and posted it in the corner mailbox so it would be gone and he couldn't have a chance to change his mind. That does it and so much the better, he thought. The truth is, Monk has had hold of my mind for too many years. I've been his man far too long. Let him be what he wants to be. He doesn't like my world. Now I'm out of his and damn glad I am. But on the way back to the house he thought, What was it about that man that I loved?

◊ SEVEN ◊

A T THE END OF THE WEEK he joined the Press Club to help convince himself he was out of the academic world. When he sat at the bar with newspapermen and television journalists he could tell they weren't sure of him; they thought he was an academic who had had some university connection with Monk, and were baffled yet amused by his manner: he acted as if he thought he owned the place. He wore blue jeans and a leather jacket, smoked a pipe and had the biggest bar bill. But soon he got the assignment from *The Star* to write of the funeral of the powerful politician, Shoemaker, a national figure whose corpse was carted solemnly across the country, stopping at every whistle stop while the good companions on the train had a great and endless drunk. Working all night on the story, Mark edited and revised, feeling that Monk was looking over his shoulder, feeling he actually had his arm around his shoulder, pointing to every unneeded word. When the story was printed Bill Soames of *The Telegram* bought him a drink at the bar. From then on he made other newspaper friends. By the time all the leaves had fallen from the trees and the colder weather came on, he no longer felt alone in the big house. In fact, he seldom was alone. A girl he had known at college, Joyce Tebbets, a tall willowy girl, a radio producer with the CBC, came one Saturday afternoon to help him rake up the last of the leaves. She stayed for dinner. They drank

cognac and listened to Janis Joplin records, and she stayed
the night and Sunday night too. But Joyce had a style that
baffled him. She had an utter gurgling abandonment. She
cupped her breast, holding it up for his lips, as if he were her
child. After they had made love she would say, "Don't you
feel better now?" Believing he was lonely in the big house,
she convinced him he ought to have a dog. She had a friend,
a woman who bred poodles, and she got him a four-month-
old standard poodle that would grow into a giant poodle in
two months, she said. They called the dog Alfie, and the
neighbours got accustomed to seeing Mark walking Alfie
around the block.

At the end of that week, walking across from the
reference library, he stopped facing the library, feeling
compelled to go in and look at the back issues of the *New
Statesman* and *The Spectator* to see what was happening in
London. He hadn't heard from Monk. He was beginning
to think he might never hear from him. Finally he found
both papers had pieces on Monk. The *New Statesman*,
turning on him savagely, said his book about Russian
people in their daily lives indicated the set of his mind
now; a deft dismissal of all socialist states as failures in
simple human relationships, because no man could be open
with another. As for Monk's sad diatribe in *The Observer*,
the *New Statesman* said, he showed he was simply bored
with freedom, a disappointed socialist ready to turn his
back on everything he and his friends had worked for. And
it should be remembered the *New Statesman* said that men
bored with freedom were always dangerous men. On the
other hand, *The Spectator*, in a piece written in the style of
a sad obituary, said that Monk's friends should not forget
that his father had been a Methodist clergyman. What had
been bred in the bone was coming out now in Monk in
this late stage of his career. Jeremy had become Jeremiah,
brooding and wailing over the sins of his own Jerusalem.

So he's really getting a punch in the nose, Mark thought with satisfaction. Well, good. He has it coming to him, and no doubt, it's why he doesn't write to me.

Though he said these things to himself, the fact was that every time he sat down to write a story he still could feel Monk behind him, full of concern, looking over his shoulder, editing him. It tormented him till he did the story Alfie, his poodle, got for him. In the mornings he used to walk Alfie over the bridge, then along Isabella to Jarvis, then back, going around the block. This was the neighbourhood called "the Track," where the hookers hung out at all hours. Indeed, it was now their turf. Turning the corner at Earl Street, he passed a young woman talking to a child who was sitting on the curb as she might have sat when she was eight years old. She looked about twelve now. Alfie stopped to nuzzle the child, who petted, then hugged him. "What's his name?" she asked, her arm around his neck. Her friend, the old prostitute, stout, thick waisted and goodnatured, said cheerfully, "I've seen you come this way before, pal. We get to know everyone." This was all in the late autumn sunlight. Profoundly moved by the little hooker kid sitting on the curb, her arm around Alfie, Mark asked the stout prostitute if they would have a coffee with him in the corner res-taurant. The kid could have some ice-cream. They came along with him. In the restaurant they talked and laughed. He asked questions and found out that there were many little kids of twelve and fourteen working as hookers along the Track. Before they parted he let the child hold Alfie's chain and walk along half a block with him. She kept saying, "Isn't he wonderful, Mister? Aren't you lucky?"

Afterwards, he couldn't get the picture of the little kid sit-ting on the curb and playing with Alfie out of his head. But the thing was that when he wrote the little story, Jeremy Monk, full of concern, was not there looking over his shoulder. Nor was he behind him, editing. The city editor said, "No one can miss on a good dog story, Didion, but my God, I think you're becoming a writer."

Late the same afternoon when it was dark outside and he was at the bar in the Press Club, big Maloney, the movie critic, came over and handed him the *New York Times Book Review*. "There's your boy, Monk," Maloney said. "I guess he's made it in the Big Apple. Give it back to me when you're finished." The review of the Russian book was warmly enthusiastic and quite long. There was also a full-page advertisement and a striking picture of Monk in the middle of the page. Never before had Monk got this kind of attention. This is it, for him, Mark thought. At last, the light had fallen on the neglected great writer and he gave *The Times* back to Maloney who was still at the corner table, and left the Press Club to walk home. It started to snow, the first snowfall of the year, the snow coming down heavily, so soft and thick in the mild air and streaming across the street lights. When he came to his bridge over the ravine the lights down below on the road were like little magic lanterns under a thick white shimmering screen changing to a glowing thicker blanket. The snow came up over his ankles. At his house, he heard Alfie's welcoming bark. When he opened the door Alfie jumped up, his paws out to him. He couldn't break Alfie of this bad greeting habit; other people didn't like it. Alfie was full-grown now, and with his long hair all combed out he looked like a giant snowball. As Mark pushed him down and away he saw, on the floor by the let-terbox, a special delivery letter. It was from Monk. Slipping off his coat he stood under the hall light reading: "The story was good," Monk wrote, "but I had told you it was, and I didn't have to say so again. Now as for my essay back there in *The Observer*, though you said little or nothing about it, I felt all your disappointment in me. It has troubled me deeply. For reasons that are not clear to me, I can't bear to

have you believe I could be someone other than the man
you thought you knew. Much time has passed, Mark. There
were things I thought you would see for yourself. Vietnam
and all, but I don't know whether you have altered your
opinion. However, I never could bear to try and explain
myself and am not going to try now. Let me remind you,
though, of our conversation about reporting. Do you
remember? The greatness of writing is in the reporting —
what is in fact observed. My *Observer* piece was simply my
report on this decade, yours and mine. It was, of course, a personal report. Was it objective? Was Flaubert objective? Was he
the most highly objective or the most truly personal of all reporters? The question you should ask is: Was there truth in the
observations? Look around and ask yourself if any of the observations were false. Remember, you said in your piece that
you thought I lived for the truth. No one has ever said anything about my work that pleased me more. I want it to be so
now. It must be so. I dearly want you to see that it is so.
Remember this. In my *Observer* piece I was clearing the
ground so that new things can be born. The new thing, Mark!
But first, Mark, we have to clear the ground and I've done it. I
have a new book planned. I expect to be seeing you soon. I
have something in mind for us."

The letter was like a soothing touch, a warm clasp of the
hand and as Mark stood musing, he tried, as he had tried
once before in Paris, to understand how Monk had come to
care so much about the view he might have of him.

The melting snow from his rubbers was making a little
puddle in the vestibule. Alfie, his tail wagging, knowing he
was to be taken out, kept ducking and sniffing at the melting
snow, looking up at Mark. But Mark, taking off his coat,
forgot about the rubbers. Hurrying up to his room and his
typewriter, he wrote a note to Monk. He told him how
delighted he was to hear from him and how exciting and
gratifying it was to hear about the new book breaking new

ground. He was exhilarated, he was excited, a young man drawn into the larger world of literature and watching a new book being born.

Nursing the unexpected elation, he put on his overcoat again, got Alfie's chain from the kitchen and opened the front door. Before them lay the snow-covered street, the snow unbroken by any footstep, and across the street, the wide lawn, all in deep snow, the street lights, too, veiled in snow. Usually, Alfie bounded out as soon as the door was opened. Now, stiffly, he looked to the right, then to the left, then half dazed and questioning, at Mark. Alfie had never seen a white world of snow. He had never seen snow. His step was hesitant. "It's snow, just snow," Mark said. "Come on, Alfie," and he led the way, the poodle taking careful, wary delicate steps. At the sidewalk, he freed Alfie from the chain. Trotting five paces to the left, Alfie, hesitating, wavering, tasting, finally buried his nose in the snow, then walked slowly and warily across the street to the wide lawn, and there, after hesitating, he took a little run to the left, then a little run to the right, then at last, a high exultant leap in the air, until, after dashing round and round crazily in a wide circle, he took an exultant celebratory roll in the snow in appreciation of its discovery and the white wonder of new soft things never seen before. Mark thought of Paris and sitting with Cretia, looking in wonder at Monet's garden. If Cretia were beside him, watching Alfie's delighted astonishment, she would say, "There. You see what I mean?"

◊ EIGHT ◊

WHILE WAITING TO HEAR from Monk, Mark kept track of his progress in New York. There, his Russian book had quickly become a best seller. Monk's first appearance on television would have been arranged by the publisher as a promotion for the book, Mark knew. But after that appearance, all the talk shows wanted him, and not just to talk about his book; they had discovered his unique personality; he could listen to a host, or another guest with an intense, sympathetic, helpful concern, then gently and with his charming smile and vast but entertaining scholarship, make the questioner look like a fumbling schoolboy. The camera loved his skull-shaped face with the tightly drawn skin, high cheekbones, hollow cheeks and sudden puckish smile. And that white hair! The use of his hands, his eloquent hands. That crown of white hair somehow gave even more vitality to his face. Again and again, watching in wonder, Mark told himself Monk must have known exactly what he was doing. As a writer, Monk had been a very private man, known only by his written words, never a personality; a man, Mark thought, who deliberately avoided the lecture platform. Yet now, as a personality, he was grimly trying to sell his book. Yet in spite of himself, Mark loved watching him; he loved him for being so entertaining; for getting laughs from his witty sallies. He was the sharp-tongued socialist who could jest about the Royal Family; they had him on for two shows about the Royals. "He's a natural," Mark said to himself. "But why don't I hear from him?"

When Monk went on the book tour, Mark lost sight of him — for weeks — for months — yet he couldn't believe Monk had forgotten about him. Then, in the third week of January, the time of the thaw when the deep snow melted and there were actually floods on the streets, he got the letter. Having returned to New York, Monk wrote, "I am continuing the book tour in Canada beginning in your city, and I have a plan that may amuse you as much as it does me. I've shown the local publisher your article on me; it impressed him. He intended to have one of the men here accompany me. I urged him to let you be my man. It would work only after we left Toronto. The publisher, Roger O'Rourke, will look after everything. He saves money letting you go west with me. So if you are free, phone the sales manager. Here's his number."

Mark immediately called New York. He had a good long talk with the sales manager about expenses and a financial arrangement. When these things were done, Mark went to see *The Star*'s city editor to tell him about travelling with Monk. Welcoming him warmly, the city editor said, "There can be a story here at the end of the trip. Monk on this country! Monk on 'Two Solitudes'. Think of it. What a chance for him to be outrageous! The wilder the better." And at the end of that week, at four in the afternoon, Mark was in a taxi on his way to the airport.

It was a mild wet day. With the thaw had come a heavy winter fog. The whole city was fogbound. He couldn't see the tops of the bank towers. Accidents on the highway, deep in slush, delayed the taxi and Mark, out of breath and just in time, arrived at the exit aisle in the terminal and waited and watched, growing tense as though he feared he might not even be recognized. The passengers kept going by him, but then at last there was Monk half hidden behind a very tall heavy woman; the white hair shone behind the woman's wide shoulder.

Monk was wearing a black-and-white-checked Burberry coat loose enough to be a cape, with a heavy pink-and-white woollen scarf twisted around his neck and hanging over his shoulder. As a porter took his bag, he looked around uncertainly; then his face lit up. "Mark," he called, hurrying forward, his arms open. The warmth of his embrace, the real, affectionate hug he gave him, surprised Mark. He felt shy and awkward. Drawing back, Monk said admiringly, "Where did you get that fur hat? Is it a Russian hat?"

"So they say. Do you like it? I got it at a sale. Well, here we go." In the short walk to the taxi stand nothing was said. It was as if after the warmth of the embrace, they knew they were strangers again until the right words were said. Mark couldn't find these words. In the taxi he said, "I had even hoped you might stay at my place. It's a big house."

"I'd have liked that, Mark. Why is it I see you in a big house? But these things have all been arranged by the publisher. I'm booked into a hotel called the Park Plaza."

"Great. It's not far from where I live."

"And we're to have dinner tonight with your publisher, a man called O'Rourke. Do you know him?"

"Everyone around here knows O'Rourke. He's a cultural director. You'll be right up his alley now."

"Now?"

"After the big New York success and especially all that television. He believes in television," Mark said.

"All that television," Monk said, half to himself. They were out on the highway in the slush and water. In that fog, the city's distant towers could not be seen; they were just shadows. If there had been sunlight, it would have been glinting on the great glass surfaces of towers. "What was it like on the road?" Mark asked. "All those bookstores. All those people."

"It was so new to me," Monk said. "It was fascinating, and the colleges — those admiring students, the handsome girls, the women. If only they had been reading me! Ah, but now they recognize me. I'm a figure, Mark."

"Well, that's what television does. Right?"

"Right. I gather you saw a lot of me."

"All I could," Mark said. "You're a natural, Jeremy. I couldn't believe it was you. I couldn't get over it," and after grinning to himself, he was silent.

Monk looked at him sharply. "Look, Mark," he said, "you have to do these things. As you well know, I, as a writer, have kept to myself. I'm a private person. In the trade I've been in the intellectual ghetto. Not many readers. Well, I now want people to read me. In this crazy system there's only one way to do it. Become a personality, a figure. People are interested only in people, Mark. Television can do it for you. If I can grit my teeth and be smarter at it than the frauds and hicks, and get my own work read, it's worthwhile, isn't it, Mark?"

"Success of any kind is always gratifying I suppose," Mark said. "I'd like to see you deal with these New York intellectuals."

"The New York intellectuals?"

"I thought you might need them."

"They only need each other."

"Are they avoiding you?"

"Oh, come on, Mark. Of course they are. They're only a little group. They live by taking in each other's washing and talking about it."

"Still, I suppose I'm trying to get used to you as a performer among the performers, and not as a writer."

"And what's the matter with that?"

"Well, as my grandmother used to say, you lie down with dogs and you get up with fleas."

"Thank you, Mark," he said crisply. "I'll have to watch myself, won't I?" There was a touch of sarcasm in his voice

and Mark knew then that Monk did not like being told what
to do. After an uncomfortable silence, Monk, apparently
realizing he had sounded condescending, said warmly, "The
view you had of my work is often in the back of my mind,
Mark."

"It's still the way I see you."

"So it should be, and never mind the television. Don't let
it ever get in the way." Still upset, Mark wondered if Monk
was reminding him of the note he had sent to London,
"What in hell are you up to?" and he was upset, too,
remembering the greeting in the terminal, the surprising
warmth of Monk's embrace and he thought, "I wonder if he
has a son somewhere, or nearly had a son or lost one, who
might have idolized him, someone of his own flesh and
blood who saw him as he wanted to be seen." Though this
came in a flash, it felt right, and Mark was deeply moved.
Putting his hand on Monk's shoulder he said, "The great
thing about your television is that even as a performer —
just a performer — you're always yourself, never giving an
inch, and wonderfully entertaining. What's wrong with
being an entertainer?" Relaxing, Monk nodded, and then
they were at ease with each other. Nothing more needed to
be said. They had turned off the highway and were going up
University Avenue, the Parliament Buildings ahead, all the
lights on. They went around the crescent and up the avenue,
and then into the hotel where the desk clerk handed Monk a
message from O'Rourke. They would have dinner at eight,
the note said, there in the hotel. "And now for a drink,"
Monk said. "Where's the bar?" They had a drink, a Scotch,
then another one and still had two hours before O'Rourke
came. Monk should have a nap before dinner, Mark said. As
for himself, he had a little work to do. So, he would go
home. He hurried, walked his dog around the block, read
the *New York Times*, the news about Vietnam. He called
Joyce and said he would tell the housekeeper to let her in

around midnight and she could stay the night. The temperature was dropping; the thaw was over. The water on the
sidewalk had turned to ice, and while watching Alfie slide
around he thought of Cretia. Monk could tell him all about
Cretia.

◊ N I N E ◊

WHEN HE GOT BACK TO the hotel, Monk was standing by the elevator as if he had just come in. He had changed his clothes. He, too, had put on a dark suit. "These dark suits. Who is this great publisher to command such respect?" Mark asked. In the elevator, Monk explained he had decided on a walk in the neighbourhood. The new dry cold air had revived him. He had gone along Yorkville and down to Bloor and had liked the area. Watching his face, Mark thought, how like him, this curiosity about everything around him!

"Oh, there's O'Rourke," Monk said when the phone rang. Should they go down to the lobby or should they let him come up to the room? he asked. They would go down. And there, waiting at the elevator, was O'Rourke, a blond giant of a man with restless blue eyes, a lean face, and a mouth that twisted when he smiled. The twist was unfair to him. O'Rourke wasn't a sinister man, just impulsive and a little pigheaded, and looking sinister only when he was trying to justify to himself some costly silly publishing venture or some new expensive mistress, or some foolish quarrel with his patient wife. He was not deferential to Monk; he was straightforward; he was hearty. There was a fine restaurant just along the street, he said, but the food and service here in the hotel dining room were just as good. As they talked, they moved along the corridor to the dining room

which was near the bar. His editor, Hannah Holmes, would
be able to join them for dessert and a brandy, he said. When
O'Rourke entered the half-filled dining room, some patrons
looked up. Here, he was known and admired, and Monk's
picture had been in the evening paper, so these patrons
smiled at O'Rourke as if they knew him, then stared at
Monk. So far, O'Rourke had paid no attention to Mark,
believing no doubt that he was a secretary, or a kind of business manager. When the red wine came, O'Rourke raised his
glass to Monk and made one of his courtly speeches. Everything was in hand, he said. There was to be a press conference, three autographing sessions in bookstores and one
special event he had arranged himself. The poet, Elmer Lan-
caster, an academic very famous in Toronto and Montreal, a
wild romantic, was to do a half-hour television interview
with Monk on the CBC. As he laid out these plans,
O'Rourke's eyes shone with a promoter's enthusiasm. Filling
the glasses with red wine, he kept growing more boyish in
his sincere belief Monk would make his publishing season.

"You say nothing to all this, Mark?" Monk asked.

"I've been waiting to hear Roger talk about the book,"
Mark said shrugging. "The book."

"Why talk about the book?" O'Rourke asked.

"Well, Jeremy wrote a book."

"And I know we'll do well with it," O'Rourke said.

"Of course. Why not?" and again he shrugged. "It's done
well in the States. However, I didn't like some of those
reviews. They missed the boat."

"What does it matter? They gave it big space. That's all
that counts, isn't it?"

"I happen to like the book, O'Rourke."

"You see, O'Rourke, Mark liked the book," Monk said
mildly. "He wants to talk about the book."

"I haven't read the book," O'Rourke said calmly.

"No?" Monk said, astonished.

"No," and then with an endearing candour O'Rourke said, "I'll tell you something, Jeremy. Something that has worked for me for years. Can I read all the titles I publish? Of course not. Anyway, I found long ago that I could fool myself reading a manuscript. I could be wrong, I found. But I learned I was never wrong if, instead of reading the book, I met the man and got the feel of him. It's an instinct now. I can feel what success I'll have with him."

"It always works?"

"Nine times out of ten it works."

"And me?" Monk asked.

"It'll work. It'll be great. I saw the aura around you. I felt it as soon as I met you, looked at you."

"Remarkable," Monk said, bemused. "Well, at least I know I'm in good hands in this country," and as he raised his glass to O'Rourke they nodded and smiled as if celebrating their discovery of each other. The discovery came so easily Mark wondered if Monk, whose glass had been filled again and again, was getting happily drunk. Mark began to laugh. For the first time, O'Rourke looked at him thoughtfully, dubiously. "Yes, I read your piece on Monk," he began, measuring him. "It's not the style I like. Too plain. I like Tom Wolfe — you know — 'short-arm fatties whose pants never crease, they just pong in and out . . .' great stuff." Looking up, he said, "Ah, here's Hannah. She'll have dessert with us. Hannah, Hannah dear."

Monk was on his feet quickly. Hannah, a beautiful small black-haired girl, had compelling brown eyes and something silken about her. Stepping toward her before he could be introduced, Monk took her hand in both his hands and raised it to his lips as if the hand gave off some special fragrance that stirred his senses. Then he held her eyes in a moment of intimate sensual warmth. "Ah, thank you," she said with her own little secret smile as she sat down. In her presence, the tone of the conversation changed. She had read the Russian book. She knew Monk's work. Though O'Rourke was left out of the conversation, he was obviously proud of his editor. He tried to engage Mark in a sensible conversation about hockey and then about skiing. Monk and Hannah, so at ease with each other, could have been alone in the room. Then they all came together for a second liqueur. Leaving the dining room, O'Rourke walked with Monk, and following beside Hannah, Mark said, "You like him, don't you, Hannah?"

"Yes, very much."

"Tell me something. What is it that is so attractive about him?"

"To a woman?"

"To you, yes."

"Oh, I think it's because he makes me feel that things come alive. Bright warm things touching me and I'm so at ease with myself. It's a very sensual feeling."

"He hardly touched you."

"And yet I feel more secure in being the kind of a woman I am — whatever that is," and she laughed. "It's as if he's there to give, and give something I need, if I really need it."

"That's odd," Mark said. "That Italian journalist, Renata, she said the same things about him."

"I read her book."

"Oh, I see."

"No, it's just me, not Renata," she said, taking his arm. "The brandy was good, wasn't it? I feel good, don't you?" At the elevator O'Rourke said, "Tomorrow. See you tomorrow. This was great. We're on our way," and they parted. "Come up to the room with me, Mark," Monk said. In the room, sitting on the bed, Monk said, "I actually enjoyed the man. But no man should be as much in the open as he is. He's a sitting duck. It's a new breed. They call our books Titles — Titles, you know." He hiccupped. Pointing to the chair, he waited for Mark to sit down, then unaware of

Mark's embarrassment he solemnly began to undress. He got his pajamas from the bureau drawer and spread them on the bed. "Yes, and what's O'Rourke's reputation around here?" he asked.

"Couldn't be higher. All his authors love him. He'll stand on his head at high noon on the corner of Bloor and Yonge if it'll help sell a book. He fascinates me."

"Well, you saw that he fascinated me, too. And Hannah? That Hannah. She's a superior woman. Oh yes, Hannah, I must see her again."

"You will. Tomorrow."

"But another time. She must find another time, Mark."

"It's you who won't have the time, Jeremy," Mark said, getting up because Monk in his pajamas and dressing gown was opening the door. He came out to the hall, too, walking slowly along to the elevator. Three women passing turned and stared. He didn't care or even notice them. "I was glad you were with me tonight, Mark," he said.

"I just listened . . . my contribution."

"You were there. Our eyes could meet. That's important."

"It's the book you're working on that's important to me. We haven't had a chance to talk about it," Mark said, then added, "As you said, now that the ground is cleared, a new freedom, remember?"

"Ground cleared just for me."

"For you, of course. For something new."

"Well," and he hiccupped. "Excuse me. The oldest things are sometimes the newest things. I'm thinking and thinking and thinking," and then, blinking his eyes, he hiccupped again. As the elevator door opened, he went lurching along the hall. About to step into the elevator, Mark turned and called, "Jeremy," and took a step after him. He wanted to ask him about Cretia. When Monk didn't turn, Mark thought, Not now while he's hiccupping.

For a few hours the next day he was free of Monk, though never out of his shadow. In the hands of the O'Rourke sales manager, Monk was going to bookstores, being driven around town so he could get an impression of the city, walking on the streets downtown, then having lunch with O'Rourke at the National Club. At home and away from him, Mark got ready for the trip through the west, even though he apparently had some time to himself. University men who knew of his association with Monk kept phoning him. Dr. Vincent Samour of Massey College asked if he couldn't come for dinner and sit at the high table. The warden of Hart House asked if Monk could find an hour for a session with students in the big music room. He could do none of these things. He had the press conference. When Mark left the house in the afternoon for the press conference, he walked about twenty paces, then turned back. There were icy winds. He got a heavy scarf; the temperature had dropped to zero, the beginning of the hard fierce winter weather, and he thought of the innocent Monk going around hatless.

Monk met the press in a small salon in the hotel. They came from radio, television, and the newspapers and sat on little folding chairs in the salon waiting for Monk to come in and stand behind a small table set up in front of the row of chairs. As soon as he appeared, he raised both hands, almost inviting applause, and then, before sitting down, he slowly and deliberately let his eyes wander from face to face, meeting eyes and holding them. Even though not a word as yet had been said, it was a performance, and Mark was astonished. Was this Monk? Or was this a public figure who could command attention by his simple presence? And what a new presence he had! The air of a bishop who knew of his power in a public place. As he took the first question he gravely repeated it, then smirked to himself. This was the man, Mark thought, who at the time of their first meeting that day at La Coupole in Paris, had been such a private man

that he had worried about being recognized! But of course
the questions as they came were not about his Russian book.
They all wanted to know what he thought of this city, their
city. Sitting back, off by himself meditating, or as Mark
thought with cynical amusement, weighing what he might
say that would get the most attention, Monk finally leaned
forward, smiling warmly, and talked about his first impressions. Of course, the city was new. All new, he said. Since it
was so new and just being built, perhaps into a great city,
how could you walk the streets and feel it had any history?
That was all right. They were lucky. They didn't have to get
rid of the past. These streets had never run with blood, nor
seen tanks rolling against barricades. Face it, it was a city
without great romantic figures. No buried Caesars. No wild
and wanton Messalinas. And black power, was it here? Yes,
and monumentally here, a great black tower. But it was a
bank, just a bank. On the other hand, he said with his
beautiful consoling smile, we should remember that fifth-
century Athens was a new city. The new thing, indeed, can
have all the charm of novelty, of something being born.
However, he went on with a troubled air, the thing that
bothered him about the city was that it had no smell. Big
cities have a smell. Rome has a smell. Some cities stink. They
have their own fascinating stink. It's the life there. Where
there is no smell, no stink, there is no life. Isn't it the same
with people? If you have the right nose you can detect on
each living person an aroma, no matter how delicate. But
alas, in our time, a billion dollars is spent on eliminating the
scent of every one of us. A people without any odour. Oh,
my god! Have they succeeded too well here? Is there only
the smell of a paper flower? But then, laughing, he opened
his arms, and seemed to embrace them all. The conference
was over. On the way out, Mark spoke to Hannah, who was
delighted. The local city editors would be very appreciative,
she said. There would be a picture, too. She went off to din-

ner with Monk. Mark did not see Monk till they met next evening at the CBC studio. The poet, a short, plump, moon-faced, fierce-eyed man, paced up and down, hyping himself, waiting for the show to begin. He had a reputation as a flamboyant master of invective.

Taking Monk aside Mark said, "I know this fellow, and I'll give you a tip; give him an opening and he'll try and make a fool out of you. But he can get rattled himself more easily. Just watch his upper lip."

"His upper lip, yes?"

"If you see it start to tremble you'll know you've got under his skin and one more deft jab and he'll blow up."

"Thank you, Mark," again using that condescending tone, and Mark wished he hadn't offered any advice.

Though married four times, the poet was always in love with someone other than his wife. Mark believed the poet liked only big-breasted women. He had read the well-known poems that celebrated the breast. When the poet shook hands with Monk, he said, "I have an advantage, Mr. Monk. I know your work. I know, too, that you don't know mine. But that's being English, isn't it?" and patting Monk on the shoulder, he laughed. But as soon as the show began, he whirled on Monk in his most celebrated flamboyant style. "I understand you are bored with freedom," he said. "Well, I am a child of this decade." The grey-haired poet had a much-married look for such a child of the times. Monk looked grave and sympathetically concerned. It was incredible to him, the poet went on, that a man of Monk's perception hadn't been able to recognize that this decade had been a unique and golden time. Something beautiful had happened. People felt free enough to let themselves come into the open. Openness! Oh, openness! The thing that he as a poet most admired in a person, was openness. The open heart. The whole impulse in song and story and pop music and memoirs was directed toward this open intimacy. Frank and full understanding of each other as had never happened in our civilization! In this new openness wonderful things had come to pass. Things long hidden came out in the open, the poet went on. Nodding sympathetically, Monk tried to interrupt as if he wanted to be helpful. Finally, he did get in a word. "Could you help me to understand some things?" he asked gently. "You know about your time far better than I do, so be patient with me. Please help me to understand why you want to be so open with people. Doesn't it scare you? Have you no very private life, but only just this public face? Have you no sacred secret domain within you? As for me, I'd be worried if I let everything hang out, as you put it. From then on, everybody would understand me completely, and with no mystery left, be bored to death with me. It's a problem, isn't it? Help me with it, please. Where have I gone wrong imagining that your hope of freedom from — from the glory of form, freedom from all discipline, from all self-respect — is also freedom to hide from the truth. Is that freedom? Is that what you want? But my friend, and you are my friend because you are a poet — in your work, in your life, you could not afford to be so self-indulgent, could you?"

In the control booth, Mark feeling uncomfortable as if his own undergraduate years were being mocked, had to laugh. But it was like reading Monk's piece in the *London Observer*. Everyone began to laugh. Everyone knew that for years the poet had been proclaiming publicly his indulgence in all kinds of sexual fantasies: he had named some of the ladies who had loved him; he had indulged himself with words. He had reveled publicly in his quarrels with his wives. He had made a profession of letting himself go. Now, looking up and seeing laughing faces behind the glass of the control room, he couldn't find words. He got rattled. "I have my Master's degree in political science," he said. "I have an M.A. in history, too, and I've lectured on Freud and Jung."

"And I never doubted your credentials," Monk said gently.

"You bet," the poet said, and sulked.

After the show, Mark and Monk and Hannah went across the street to the Hampton Court bar. It was to be Monk's last night in town. Hannah in her black dress high on her throat, her wide-set eyes soft and melancholy, sat in her silken silence, smiling at Monk, a woman waiting, secure in her waiting. In high good humour after the debate, Monk kept saying they should have asked the angry-eyed poet to have a drink with them. "No, I've had a drink with him," Hannah said, making a face. Then she excused herself and went to the washroom. Watching her go, watching the little sway of her hips, Monk said, "Tell me something, Mark. As I went from city to city across the continent I noticed that the women seemed to be so much more cultivated than the men. Is it this way in your country too? Are they really that much smarter? I've been at parties at big homes and it seemed to me that the men were always holding back, smiling, as if all things of the mind were now the woman's department. The men provided the home and the money. Is it that way around here?"

"Well, at a big party I suppose it is. The men used to like to get together in the kitchen. The women used to like to huddle in the living room. But not now. Not around here."

"But right across the country?"

"You'll be able to see for yourself."

"Ah, yes, starting tomorrow."

"Is tomorrow too soon?" Mark asked, because Monk was eyeing Hannah as she came toward them, her eyes on Monk alone.

"I'm not quite sure," Monk said slowly. "Maybe it's just about the right time to leave." Then turning suddenly, he said, "Remember Cretia?"

"Cretia? Of course I remember Cretia," Mark said.

"She asked to be remembered to you."

"She did? We've never talked about Cretia. Come on, let's go. Tell me about Cretia."

"We'll have lots of time on the plane," Monk said, his arm going easily around Hannah as they walked to the door, and as she snuggled against Monk, walking to the door, Mark had a hunch that when she parted from him, she would be left with a warm glowing certainty that everything about her from her toes to her nipples to the lobes of her ears had delighted all his senses. At the door, they drew back turning up their collars against the icy wind. "Here, Jeremy, take my fur hat and keep it," Mark said. "You'll need it. I have another one and I took this western trip about two years ago and they told me what it's like in the winter."

"But I never wear a hat."

"Not even in Russia?"

"It was summer in Russia. Here's our taxi." Mark put his fur hat back on his own head. He would have liked to have seen Monk wearing his hat.

◊ T E N ◊

I N THE AIRPORT BAR, THEY were having the few drinks that would help them to doze in their seats on the plane. They had the local papers; they laughed, reading about the best-selling author and television personality, Jeremy Monk, and his strange and striking view of the city that had no smell of its own, in fact, no smell at all. There were interviews with some of the city fathers, who, to a man, took the Monk observations as a great compliment, a recognition that they lived in the cleanest city on the continent. Both papers had good pictures of Monk. His books weren't mentioned.

"Good lord," Mark said. "Are you on the road to becoming bigger than your books?" The main thing was, Monk said, they had given him good space. That was all that mattered.

When they were on the plane sitting together, Mark waited for a chance to look into little secret corners of Monk's life. After an hour of dozing, Monk, turning, said, "How dull this would be if you weren't with me." He was looking out at the endless expanse of snow. "Snow all the way now," Mark began. "Ice and snow," and then he remembered the instructions he had given the housekeeper about looking after Alfie, and walking him at night when it was snowing; would she remember not to let him off the leash? He could see her opening the door, letting him out and just hoping he would return. If she did this, Alfie would wander off, liking the snow, and not come back for hours.

"What's on your mind, Mark?" Monk asked.

"Nothing," he said. "Well, yes. Remember you asked if I remembered Cretia? Of course I do," and he smiled. "But I was just thinking. What do I know about Cretia?"

"Cretia. Well, let me see. You looked at those Monet paintings with her. Remember?"

"It was her idea. Yes. And I know she rides a motorbike."

"Ah, that motorbike, yes."

"A bike and a leather jacket."

"Like so many of them now. Ah, no Mark, those girls could never understand Cretia. She's out of another world. A temperament not of our time. In spite of the bike."

"What a way of putting it. You can't talk like that now!"

"More's the pity."

"What about Cretia?"

"It's, somehow, a glimpse of another time in her. I suppose you'd call her a European. Yes," he said, a little smile on his face as he kept on looking out the window. They were flying above clouds that looked like great rows of snowbanks with little valleys darkly shadowed, the crests of the snowbanks all sun tipped. Then Monk told him about Cretia's mother, the actress, the Irish woman, marrying the well-off Italian and how they had lived in a fine apartment in Parioli, which he called Mussolini's Rome, and how she had an uncle who was a bishop, and how she had spent time going to school in England and then had gone to Paris to paint. "Has she any talent for painting?" Mark asked.

"Maybe not much," Monk admitted, hesitating. "What's interesting is the way she thinks about painting." Pondering, then frowning, he said, "I think the real talent is Cretia herself. I was aware of it, I think, the first time I met her. A talent, somehow strangely singular. How to describe it? How did I describe it to myself?" His head dropped back on the little pillow on the seat provided for the neck, his eyes closed. He was drowsy, a beautiful way to fall asleep on a plane, Mark thought, trying to define what is singular about a lovely young woman. Then he heard Monk murmur, his eyes still closed, "And her face, Mark. Do you remember her face? At first glance not really beautiful, too unfamiliar, then later it comes to mind, always later. Another face becoming more mysterious. But of what time? Things long past, very real to her, I think. She's not dreamy. Oh, no, not light-headed. A flower child on a motorbike? Ah no! What is it in her glance, her walk, that makes things come close and more wonderously real? That's the thing, isn't it? Well, I think I know."

Mark, astonished, his head back on his own little pillow, thought, "This is charming. Like a man remembering how he felt when he was young. Maybe when Cretia looked at him she really made him feel young." Yet Monk went on. "I can see her coming at us, a girl out of the Middle Ages. Maybe the fourteenth century, Italy." Full of wonder now, Mark thought, Is he half asleep? Is he dreaming? Monk at his age, sixty-two, couldn't know Cretia, couldn't even know her as well as he himself did when he had his arms around her waist and kissed her. Half dozing and simply indulging himself, Monk created a Cretia, doing it with a loving touch, a smile of recognition on his face at each deft new touch he put on the painting. "Yes, the fourteenth century," he went on. "That wildness of fancy, a time so earthbound, though they believed so fervently in heaven. A look can come in Cretia's eyes — utter fierce faith. She'd go all the way, Mark, all of her all the way — if things were made real for her — her kind of real." The murmuring voice became a garbled whisper; his mouth hung open; he was asleep. Sitting up, Mark looked at Monk's face as he slept; little lines around the corner of the mouth, fine wrinkles under the eyes, look-ing older, as if in slumber his extraordinary vitality was all withdrawn. A sixty-two-year-old man dreaming of a young girl he could know only in his dream of her, a last flicker of the flame of youth. Those real girls like Hannah, he could hold them in his arms so easily, but a sixty-two-year-old man enchanted, and maybe for the last time, by a young girl he could know only in his fancy. What a way to grow old, Mark thought, listening to the heavy breathing.

The stewardess, coming down the aisle, saw the sleeping Monk and asked Mark in a whisper if he wouldn't also like another pillow. After she put it behind him he lay back and soon fell asleep. A voice from the cockpit, giving passengers the location of the plane, woke him. It was twilight with the late sun shining on great shadowy bush country and wide flat stretches of snow. Waking Monk, Mark said he regretted it was winter. In the summer or fall they would have been able to look down and see that it was a magnificent lake country. He remembered it as the land of lakes, a chain of lakes in the great woods, reaching almost to the prairie, but now the lakes looked like flat fields of snow set down in the bush.

It was dark when they got to Winnipeg. At the airport, and looking for a taxi, they agreed it didn't seem to be as cold as it was back east. There was no wind and the air was lighter, drier, yet when they got out of the taxi at the Fort Garry Hotel, they both began to shiver. At the desk, a middle-aged man in a fur coat who had been waiting, approached Monk. He was quite dignified, aware that he might be intruding, and he introduced himself as C. Parker of the Wheat Pool. He had heard on the radio that Jeremy Monk was arriving; having read about him, he said he "admired his stand" — that he believed Monk had renounced everything in the communist world. "We'd be honoured if we could put you up at the Manitoba Club," he said. How fine that would have been, Monk explained, with a quiet courtesy that matched Mr. Parker's. He said that he would only be in town for two days and the hotel was better for him because he expected to be running in and out, never knowing when. The Wheat Pool man shook hands warmly and left.

They went to their rooms. They ate in the hotel. After dinner, Mark, alone in his room, got a call from the university president, Henry Holloway, who had taught him history in his undergraduate days in Toronto. Holloway wanted Monk and Mark to have dinner with him tomorrow night. Mark knew the publisher would certainly want him to accept, and he did. When Mark joined Monk in his room, they had drinks from the bottle of Courvoisier Monk had brought with him. Monk drank too much. Yet, in the morning, looking pale and bored, he was ready to go to work. At the radio station, he brightened up. The interviewer's questions made him want to laugh and make jokes. Then, he looked bemused, and later, at the television station, he appeared to be stunned.

"The radio girl, the television girl, neither one had read a line I had written," he said. "The television girl held up the Russian book, which she hadn't had time to read, but knew it was about turning my back on communism, as she said. 'Oh, no,' I said, but glassy-eyed, she went on with her speech anyway. But you see, I had been preceded on her program by a talking mynah bird. She could still hear the words the bird said. I couldn't. But why not? I'm only another talking bird. The truth is, I've run into this all over the place."

Later in the afternoon, he saw reporters from the two newspapers who had read his remarks about Toronto having no smell of its own, and they both wanted to know if he had caught the smell of Winnipeg. They wanted to talk about city smells. He told them blandly that in their city the air was too light, too dry, too cold, for smells. It seemed to Mark, listening, that it was impossible to get him to take offence. Though he remained bright, smiling and courteous, his blue eyes told Mark he was storing away his contempt and measuring everyone. One of the reporters said to Mark, "He's a great guy, isn't he? Most of these mucky-muck intellectuals are always looking down their noses. What book of his do you think I should read?" When they had gone, Mark asked, "How do you do it, Jeremy?" and Monk said, "It all helps, Mark. Radio, television, newspapers, all building up the name. But the name doesn't make them read you. It's maddening, but I'm tired of the intellectual ghetto. I want to be read."

"But look here, Jeremy," Mark said. "In the beginning, I don't think you cared whether such people read you. Try asking them who they read. That'll fix you."

"Everyone who writes wants to be read," he said. "And now for our university president."

At first glance, Mark hardly knew this man who had once been his history teacher, and who, plump and affable in a grey lamb hat and double-breasted fawn overcoat, came forward to embrace him like an old close friend. In fact, they had never much liked each other. As a young history professor Holloway had been irritable, easily wounded and short-tempered — if questioned. But having decided to become an academic politician, a man who was often mentioned as a Conservative political leader, he had acquired a vast YMCA good humour. His manner invited all the help you could give him in the name of hearty good fellowship while he made his way shrewdly from smaller presidencies to bigger ones. "Ah, Jeremy Monk," he said. "What a pleasure. You've taught me how to use the language accurately. You've taught me that when the language is debased, as it is now, and words lose their meaning, our society is in deep trouble." Monk knew he wasn't dealing with a fool.

The president took them to the Manitoba Club for dinner. It was a comfortable club, but of another cosier and more easily opulent time. At dinner, the president talked about the new Europe, drawing Monk out while listening intently. Then he said he wanted to walk them to the nearby house of a Professor Livingston, a history teacher with whom he was in sharp disagreement about the future of Europe. "Livingston is a stubborn man," he said. "An Englishman who has forgotten he is an Englishman and thinks that England is simply part of Europe, always was, and now must rejoin Europe — if it is to have any future. Well, that goes against my whole view of the motherland. You're an Englishman, Monk. What do you think? I mean as a socialist? There are some socialists around here," he said chuckling. "I'll learn things if you get talking to Livingston."

Then, as a man whose world included more than politics, he asked, "Did you really know James Joyce in Paris? What about Sartre? I've read Simone de Beauvoir. Was Sartre a likeable man, or a strange little fellow who couldn't really make love to a woman?" Monk humoured him, charming him with bits of gossip about Paris intellectuals. Listening to him, Mark said, tongue in cheek, "With you two, I can believe I'm back in Paris in a café on a sunlit day." Indeed, he could believe it till they put on their coats and stepped out to the street. The temperature had dropped sharply. It was at least twenty-five below zero, and Mark, his arm under Monk's, felt him shivering as they walked, still talking about Paris. Suddenly, he touched one of his own ears because it felt peculiar. It didn't feel like his own ear.

Stopping, he quickly pulled down the fur cap, then looked at Monk, hatless, his white hair blowing, his ears white, too. Maybe he was too cold over his whole body to think of his ears, and talked on and on as if finding some warmth in his own words. "Jeremy," Mark said. "Wait." He pulled out of his pocket heavily padded earmuffs he had kept for the always hatless Monk. "Back in Toronto I thought of your ears, Jeremy," he said. He clamped the muffs over Monk's ears. "Your ears could fall off and you wouldn't know it."

"I thought they had already fallen off," he said. "Oh, my guardian angel," and he squeezed Mark's arm gratefully. The smiling president, his big fur hat over his ears, his heavy scarf wrapped around his throat and secure in his long woollen underwear, had walked on ahead. Now he turned, waiting. "You've got to get used to it," he called cheerfully, then he talked on about the last time he was in Paris and where he had eaten, a human voice in the country Jacques Cartier had called the land of Cain. "How far?" Mark asked, his teeth chattering.

"Just two blocks," said the president. No more was said. It was as if Monk and Mark, holding back words, held on to the last of the warmth in them. Then, stopping suddenly, Monk looked up at the northern sky with its great flashing ribbons of Northern Lights, green, yellow and red. "Never in my life have I been so cold. Why? Is it the wild lights?"

Mark said, "You've got to get used to it — like the president said. Do you know those lights in this cold could drive you mad? Maybe our president is mad. Are you mad, Dr. Holloway?"

"If I am, I'm used to it. We're all used to it," he answered. "You even get to like it."

At last, they were at a neat house with snow banked high on the path and snow up to the window. The house with every light on was shining warm and bright. While the president rang the bell they stood shivering on the stoop. Then, the door swung open, wide open, and they were met by a blast of warm air. The stunning shock, the thick heavy blanket of warm air, wrapped around them, surprising in its sudden luxurious comfort, an unexpected sensual pleasure such as Mark had never enjoyed. "Hold me, hold me, let me swoon to death," Mark cried. Then, they were laughing in the hall, all laughing! Professor Livingston, a short bald Englishman in a tweed jacket, took their coats. Monk said, "I'm alive again. Life is soothing. Life is wonderful," and he embraced Mrs. Livingston, six feet tall, blonde and English, who was offering him a glass of brandy.

Two bearded faculty members the same age as Monk were sitting around a brightly burning grate fire: steady-eyed Barnet, from the economics department, and McNeice, thin, sad-eyed with a scholarly stoop, from the history department. When they were all seated, making a half-circle around the fire, the president, cheery and smiling, always smiling, began to tell about the conversation he had had with Monk and Mark at dinner about England having no future outside Europe. The president assumed the air of a man who expected to hear brilliant debate between Englishmen, Monk and Livingston. Looking irritated, Livingston pointed at the president, but before he could speak, the short bearded man, Barnet, who had been leaning forward eyeing Monk intently, held up his hand. "Excuse me for just a minute," he said, and then to Monk, "You don't remember me? But how could you?"

"Barnet, you say?"

"Yes, Barnet."

"No," said Monk, looking baffled. "Where was it?"

"Madrid. Toward the end," Barnet said. "The International Brigade. I heard of you, Monk. You were a thorn in someone's side, and on the run at the end, I think."

"You were there? This is incredible," Monk said.

"Yes, POUM and that Stalinist general."

"I was tipped off," Monk said. "Madrid, oh, Madrid," and transfixed, he stared at the glowing fire.

The other bearded man, tired and stooped, said quietly, "I was there, too. The Mackenzie-Papineau Brigade they called us."

"My God," Monk said. "That we should be here and alive. Men like you, they came from all over. Young men ready to die," and he glanced at the president, upset, as if he knew the historian had planned this for his benefit. Sinking into his chair, the president tried to smile and nod approvingly. He could do this by habit, no matter how full of disapproval he was. He believed that these bearded men had long ago put aside their left-wing loyalties. They had been given tenure. Now, listening to their eager voices as they remembered, and watching their changing faces, he could hardly conceal his uneasy astonishment. The light of youth was in the eyes of men he thought he knew, the light of youth as they talked to Monk. Their tone changed, their faces changed. Full of bitterness, they talked about how England and the United States had betrayed democratic Republican Spain, a sellout to Hitler and Mussolini and Franco, while the lights from flames flickered over their bearded faces. Standing up, Monk went to speak, but there was a catch in his throat. He seemed to have forgotten who was there. His arms went out to the bearded men, who also stood up. They embraced warmly. "Ah, but the bitterness is still there, isn't it?" Monk asked.

"When I remember, yes," said the grave, stocky man.

"I try to remember. I try not to forget," his colleague said. "I suppose history always makes a man bitter. History always makes bitter reading."

"I don't know," Monk said. "Bitterness can at least remind us of what we once had, what we thought were the only things worth dying for."

"And here we are, forgetting what we thought we lived for. Man's fate. Yes."

"Maybe it was the last great cause?" Monk said. "I mean, there was a clear line. The just cause."

"I think it was," Livingston said, startling the president, for Livingston was known as a very conservative historian.

"Well, it was where, as a very young man, I learned that injustice so often triumphs," Monk said, sitting down. Looking into the fire, meditating, his thoughts turned inward and his silence became so profound that no one dared break in on it. The light and shadows from the changing flames gave a beauty to his white head and a mysterious gravity to his face. Then Mark thought he saw a tear on Monk's cheek. Turning slowly to him, Monk said, "Mark, when I was a small boy my mother used to say, 'Thrice armed is he whose quarrel is just.' Well, it isn't so, Mark. Yet, as these men, my comrades of those times, know — everything seemed so clear to us. We were young in heart. There's that to remember, always to remember."

Suddenly, Mark was fiercely proud of him, so proud he glared at the president and nearly made a fool of himself by reminding the president he had never liked him. "Good men," Mark said, nodding to Monk. "Good men. I'll be all right while I, too, can remember. What a dead world it is when people can't bear to remember things. I know I'll have a good life if I can bear to remember things. This is a great evening."

The bearded men said, "Hear. Hear." Livingston had an amused, satisfied smile. The president, having thought it over, was beaming again. Yes, it was a good evening for such a bitter cold night. In the morning, Mark went out early to a department store and bought two sets of long underwear.

I
T SNOWED ALL NIGHT. IN
the morning, it was still
snowing and at the airport the planes weren't taking off. Two
hours later, when Mark called, it was the same thing, no break
in the overhead, no visibility. It was snowing so hard that they
had to take the train, and soon were rolling across the prairies
on the way to Regina in a dim grey light with the low sky and
the white land all one, and snow streaming across the train
windows. Before leaving the hotel, they each had two Bloody
Marys and now, out of breath from rushing, they dozed, leaning against each other and swaying together when the train
rolled. Few passengers were in the car. When he opened his
eyes, Mark saw that Monk, wide awake, was staring out the
window as if in a trance. "Jeremy," he said, "Jeremy."

"Eh? Oh yes. What?"

"What's on your mind? Looking out there."

"I wasn't looking out there."

"Good. There's nothing out there."

"No, I was thinking of us coming out of that bitter bone-
chilling cold. Coming into that unbelievable soothing
warmth. The relief! The orgasmic shock of it. The unadul-
terated sensual shock."

"It was something, all right. I'll never forget it."

"Thinking about that took me back. Maybe because of
those comrades with the beards, I thought of the time I
tried to commit suicide."

"You! Suicide! Not you, Jeremy. Come on."

"You forget the times, Mark, and what had happened. It was just after the civil war in Spain. I'd got into France, I didn't want to go home to England, fat old complacent England so blind to what was coming. I was young, a Marxian socialist, but also an idealist, and now I was without a cause. Injustice in the saddle everywhere. I was in Paris trying to earn a living sending off pieces to the English papers. A few things were printed. I was starving. I was terribly disappointed in the world and in myself, that deep disappointment! My nerves were shot. I think I must have been having a nervous breakdown. I was seeing everything too clearly. Hitler and the war! Any fool could have seen it coming in Spain. I thought they must have wanted it to come. I couldn't sleep. Nights without sleep, just the dark and disappointment in the dark. Trying to put myself to sleep, I made up rhymes. I had read that the most soothing words in the language were 'cellar door,' I said them over and over in the dark. Then words that went with cellar door. Lady Ottoline Mellor. I knew it should have been Morell but I wanted the 'or' sound. You must have heard of Lady Ottoline Morell."

"One of Bertrand Russell's lady friends?" Mark asked.

"Yes, a decade ahead of me. I used to read about her fabulous red hat and her manor house. When very young, I used to dream that I too had been invited to the manor house. Over the years, her strange name must have stuck in my head. Well, cellar door, cellar door. I remember the words building up night after night till it went like this: 'Lady Ottoline Mellor, listening at the cellar door, heard the wanton Eleanor's footsteps in the corridor. Coming closer — one step more, and she was at the open door. But Lady Ottoline Mellor said, no, you don't, you little whore, and slammed and locked the cellar door. And heard the cry from Eleanor. The one wild cry and nothing more. Cellar door, cellar door.' Hungry, overwrought, betrayed, I remember I thought I'm here in this room suffering. I only have to open a door and I'm in another room. Just as easy as that. Just open a door. I took a big overdose of sleeping pills. I was out for a long time. I woke up vomiting, then shivering and so cold. As cold as I was the other night. I longed for some warmth — to come in from the cold. If I could have come into the ecstatic warmth we felt the other night, out of the cold, wrapped in the warm blanket of life. I thought it had to be somewhere. See, Mark. I lived."

"I see."

"Finally, I went back to England."

"To live for the truth?"

"There's power in it, Mark, and life, too."

"There's a power in you now, Jeremy."

"I don't know. Maybe. For the truth as I see it," and with his puckish grin, looking out the window, he said, "and I can't see much of anything out there, although it's getting lighter. The snow is stopping, the sun's trying to come out. My God, look! What's that? Am I dreaming?" and they saw, in the last of the snow, the wild white horses running free, a herd of them a hundred yards away, racing along, tossing their heads, their snow-covered bodies, just for a minute touched by a gleam of sunlight, then fading away, becoming just shadows lost in swirling snow. "Is that real?" Monk asked.

"They roam the prairies," Mark said. "The wild horses." The wild horses had stirred his own imagination. Racing where? To a death somewhere. He could hear Monk saying, "It's so easy, just open a door, then you are in another room." But what did it have to do with wild horses in the prairie snow? Then Monk said, "I was thinking of Hannah and a look on your face as you watched her. I don't know how it was with you growing up, but I'm sure you were raised in that dark Christian shadow about the whole sexual experience. Am I right? Well, it's a Christian aberration. The great St Augustine, a remarkable man, called woman a temple over a sewer. Imagine! That dreadful Church father, Tertullian, called her the gateway to hell. I think all this would have astonished the Galilean. It certainly didn't come from him. Think of Mary Magdalene. Closer to him than any of them. The Galilean seems to have liked women. No, the nonsense started about the end of the first century when frantic Christians believed the end of the world was really at hand. They really believed it. Therefore, the sexual blessing, the ecstasy that the great pagans celebrated as a religious rite, a bounty from the gods, was irrelevant. It was a bondage. It was really abstinence that was freedom. Well, the world didn't end, but the aberration was dignified as Christian asceticism. And I think this denial of our nature is a sad, pathetic, impudent rebuke to our creator."

"I don't know. . . I . . ." Mark began, then was too astonished to go on. Monk didn't sound like a Marxian, a scientific socialist. What had happened to him? The old question. Then he remembered that Monk had had a clergyman for a father; these ancient Christian waters run deep in many old socialists. Ideas he had learned about in his boyhood might always be deep in the back of Monk's mind. As for the women like Hannah, Monk hadn't tried to seduce them. They were part of the sensual world that delighted him. He bestowed his warmth on women and went on his way, and they, afterwards untroubled, and loyal to him, went on their own way. A little in awe of him, Mark thought: He has an understanding of women, all women, that I can never have. It's his nature, the wonder of the sensual. Women don't care how old he is. He's a wonder. Then growing perplexed, he thought: Yet, he knows nothing really about Cretia. Just the obvious banal facts, a figment of his imagination, she satisfies him. Why am I so sure I know so much more about her than he does? A feeling between Cretia and me. It's there. I felt it. Monk's blue eyes were on him. "Someday," Mark said, "you may say something I don't believe. When you start doing it, I think I'll start letting you know, Jeremy."

"My boy, that's what I'm counting on," he said, and this was just before they arrived in Regina, tired out and ready for bed.

In the morning, they did the same dull things they did in Winnipeg; the radio interview, the amusing if witless talk with a girl on television and Monk delighting them all as a personality. Then came the round of the bookstores and a newspaper interview. It was getting a little milder. When they were leaving Monk's room for the airport and the plane to Calgary, Mark said, "Wait a minute, Jeremy," and he drew Monk over to the window. He knew Monk had no impression at all of Regina and might not even remember he had been on the prairies. The window, high in the hotel, looked out over a vast endless snow-covered plain all the way to the horizon. "I remember when I was here. It was in the late summer," Mark said, "and I stood at one of these windows. It was quite a sight out there. Reaching to the horizon, the ripening wheat, a magnificent cloth of gold, rippling a little in the wind, and this became a town set in a golden bowl."

"Thanks, Mark," Monk said drily. "I'll remember."

"Jeremy, don't patronize me," Mark said sharply. "I'm trying to tell you something."

"I'm sorry, Mark. That's me," he said startled. "Forgive me. I must be in a hurry to get out of town."

Things were the same in Calgary, a town that boomed between depressions. Houses and buildings were not well kept, even a little shabby. But oil prices were beginning to rise. People had started to come from the east. Welcomed as a public figure, Monk played his role with great dignity and the air of a cardinal extending his hand to be kissed. He even said a few words at the Petroleum Club where he had been taken by the leading bookseller. When they went on to Edmonton, they made the same rounds. Since the same things were always happening, they weren't sure where they were. His nose in the air, Monk said, "Don't forget to remind me I have been in Edmonton." He became himself only on the plane on the way to Vancouver, flying over the Rockies. The plane circled for half an hour near the landing area to be used if there was terribly stormy weather ahead. Staring raptly at the vast mountain slopes, his imagination stirred, Mark wondered why they were so forbidding, so alien even to mountain men, and he wondered, too, if Napoleon or Hannibal could ever have marched men through those passes as they had done through the Alps. Then, suddenly, the plane seemed to be dropping out of the sky; they were out of the Rockies and into a country of green hills with a deep shadowed valley, mysterious in mist from gently falling rain, and Monk said happily that there could be troll kings and elves in these hills, and he asked it if were true that at this time of year the crocuses were blooming in Vancouver.

◊ TWELVE ◊

As YET THERE WERE NO crocuses in Vancouver, but there was a soft rain with moments of sunlight, then mist and a glimpse of a white-capped mountain far beyond the British Properties over the bridge. The waters of English Bay and the Pacific did not look like the eastern waters of the Atlantic Ocean. This had to be a delusion, Mark thought; maybe it was only the light that was different. Yet the Pacific oysters were different, weren't they?

There was a strength in Monk, a presence as a public figure, and Mark marvelled at how easily he had come to rely on this power. In a twenty-minute talk he gave to the Junior Board of Trade meeting in the Hotel Vancouver where they were staying, he talked about the city they had toured by car. He called it a city of conjecture in a country of conjecture. The fine fingers of Asia reached here, he said, but those great trees in Stanley Park were here before our world began and might be here after it vanished. Timeless as the hookers on the streets. Why were there so many hookers here? Ships that had come into the harbour? Hookers liked harbour cities, he said. Then he spoke about freedom and disorder and about the slob world we lived in, and shabby men and shabby women, matted long hair, and marijuana. Yet he loved the Beatles, he said. Their music was light and gay. It astonished Mark that he did not bother to talk about his books. Maybe he felt he didn't need to now that he had become a presence. His timing was masterly. His long silences in which his head was held at a meditative angle, were magnetic. He was in turn witty, amusing, then changing, an emperor of the mind who had good-naturedly deigned to appear at lunch with the local tradesmen. It was astonishing, too, that he could remain so beautifully himself. The booksellers loved him. Both *The Sun* and *The Province* printed his picture. The Russian book was selling in the local stores. He had many invitations to private homes, which Mark declined.

On the third night, having left Monk in the bar, Mark was in his room working on expense accounts. He paid all the bills. Then, he found himself looking idly out the window. It had rained all afternoon, but now there was moonlight and he could see that snow-capped mountain shining in the dark, the snow cap resting on a formation called "The Sleeping Beauty." As the moonlight on the mountain worked on his imagination, he believed he could see a shining white woman in her mountain dress, and he thought of Monk talking about women. But with all his long experience, why did he have to fantasize about Cretia? Why did he have to make up his own picture of her? Was it because she was still as far away from him as the Sleeping Beauty reposing there in the mountain, something to stir an elderly man's fancy in the moonlight? Any woman, seen in the light you wanted to see her. Then the telephone rang and Monk, calling from his own room which was on the floor above, asked, "Are you busy, Mark?"

"No. What's on your mind, Jeremy?"

"I have someone here with me. I'd like you to meet her."

"Why? Why me?"

"It's interesting. Look, we'll be right down."

Prepared as he was for some exotic beauty, or a fascinating intellectual lady Monk had encountered in the bar, Mark put on his jacket. The knock came; he let them in; first Monk with his amused, questioning smile, then a woman of thirty, stocky, square faced, blonde, in a leather jacket, her cheeks bursting with health. "Meet Miss Matulak," Monk said.

"How do you do, Mark," she said, gripping his hand firmly.

"Sit down," Mark said, taken aback by her heartiness and friendly grin. Monk, who had brought his bottle of brandy with him, went into the bathroom for glasses.

"Do you live in town, Miss Matulak?" Mark asked.

"Yeah. This is home," she said. "How about you? It's Toronto, I understand."

As Monk, who had brought only two glasses from the bathroom, poured the drinks, he said, "It's all right, Mark. She doesn't drink. Let you and me drink to Miss Matulak."

"Gladly," Mark said. "Here's to you, Miss Matulak."

"To our friendship," she said smiling. "Our new friendship."

"Yes, friendship," Monk said, and after he had made sure Miss Matulak was comfortable in her chair, he moved his own chair close to her. "Miss Matulak can't stay too long. The taxi. She has a taxi, Mark."

"That's true and I'm really sorry. I can't stay long," she said. "You see, I've parked the taxi. It's been there for an hour. That's far too long. I'll get a ticket."

"It's her own taxi," Monk explained.

"And it's how I met Jeremy," she said. "Well, isn't this great? Imagine," she said, "Jeremy from London and Paris, and you from Toronto."

"It's like this," Jeremy began, then hesitated, half confused himself about how he had come to be there with Miss Matulak. "I was in her taxi. It got stuck on a mud road. We got talking and afterwards I asked her in for a drink."

"You see," she explained to Mark, "when you drive a taxi you don't sit at the hotel bar. So we sat in Jeremy's room. Anyway, I don't drink."

"So we were having a coffee and a sandwich in my room," he said.

"And becoming real good friends," she said.

"Yes, friends. To have friends everywhere," Monk said with his bemused air, watching Mark's face. Turning to her, he said, "I know you'll like Mark, and I know he'll want to be a friend, too. Tell him about your friends."

"Not close friends," she said modestly, "though some people would call us pen pals. Now and then some good guy gets in the taxi and we get talking and know we could be friends. I could tell it about Jeremy here, and Jeremy said I'd like you, Mark. I do, too. How about it?" and she put out her hand. Again the firm grip. Her square healthy face was shining with honest goodwill. As Mark met her honest eyes, he was afraid to smile, or make any remark that would sound patronizing. "Oh, you're right. I know we can be friends," he said, "and now I'd like to know something about you."

"It'll all come out," she said, leaning back comfortably. "Now to begin? Well, I live with my father. He has a little tobacco shop."

"And you have a taxi, I see. Were you born here?"

"Oh, no. The prairies. My father was what you called a sodder. Years ago, he built one of those sod houses. After my mother died it got lonely. Even watching the moon rise on the prairies can make you feel lonely. Lovely but lonely. Then the winters. The prairie winters. So my father came here."

"And it's not lonely here?"

"Good lord, no. Not when you're friendly."

"You write to your friends?"

"Not if they don't write back. It's surprising, though," she said, her head on one side as she pondered. "All kinds of people from all over come to Vancouver. I guess it isn't really surprising that so many of them want to have a friend here. I expect if they ever come here again they'll look me up. They come from all over the world, like Jeremy." After glancing at her watch she jumped up. "My taxi," she said. "It'll have a ticket on it. Now look, Jeremy. You're great, but I want you to promise me something. Before you leave tomorrow morning come into the tobacco shop. I want to give you and Mark a cigar. Right?"

"Right," Mark said.

"Right," Jeremy said. "Well, I'll walk you down to the taxi," and taking the smiling girl's arm, he walked her out. Ten minutes later he was back in the room. "Well, there's an exotic for you," he said, still baffled. "I can't believe it."

"How come, Jeremy? You and that girl?"

"It's as she said, just as she said, Mark, and I can't believe her."

"Come on. What happened?"

In the bar, he said, a Chinese student from the university had spoken to him. The student, a socialist or a Chinese communist, who had read all his books, wanted him to visit some of his Chinese Marxist friends. The student, who had to leave, gave him his address. "I was curious about these Chinese Marxists," Monk said. "Well, after waiting an hour, I got into a taxi, Miss Matulak's taxi, and drove out to a new suburb, and we were wobbling along slowly on a road that was muddy and deep in ruts. The moon was out, but the road was awful and we couldn't find the address on that street of new houses, some quite small. But we finally found the address and, of course, there were no lights in the house. No one came to the door. Maybe I had the wrong address. I got back in the taxi and the wheels spun and we were stuck in a deep mud rut. I got out to push. She rocked the car. I kept pushing and wondering when I'd have the heart attack. She got out and we both pushed. She got in again, rocking, and finally the cab rolled out of the rut. Exhausted as I was, I sat beside her, closing my eyes and she began to talk to me. She didn't know who I was. Never heard of me. Said she knew I was a kind man and liked me very much and wanted to be my friend. What she was up to I didn't know. Since she couldn't go into the bar she came up to my room and then, well, you heard her. What's she up to, Mark? What's she after?"

"Nothing. Just friendship."

"But it's absurd. In the room I couldn't touch her."

"She's a natural. Just what she is, a natural."

"Are you sure?" he asked.

"Of course I'm sure."

"Well. Perhaps so. Perhaps so," he said dubiously. "You see I thought, there she is alone in my room with me, a fine prairie flower never near a man except her father, never a man in her bed. The prairie hunger in the lonely prairie woman and she likes me."

"And then no sexual feeling at all?"

"None at all, Mark. None at all."

"Just friendship. Perfect friendship."

"I had to see what you thought," he said. Then half to himself, he murmured, "Incredible! Simply incredible!"

"How can so wise a man be so bemused?" Mark asked, and then laughed.

"Don't laugh; this is an event," he said, shrugging. "All places, all cities should give you something to remember, and now I know that wherever I am and hear of a city on the west coast called Vancouver, I'll think of that girl. Just that girl. The natural. Good night, Mark."

"Good night, good Jeremy."

In the morning on the way to the airport, they visited the tobacco store of Miss Matulak's father. In a solemn rite, they took down Miss Matulak's address and gave her theirs. She presented both of them with fine Cuban cigars. They shook hands warmly.

When they arrived in Toronto they met with O'Rourke, who, though only a few weeks had passed, looked older, more flushed and dissipated. He had all the reports from the west and all the clippings and they were great, he said. The general interest in Monk's personality had so delighted him he had decided that he, himself, would go with Monk to Ottawa and Montreal and Mark would not be needed. Next day, Mark drove Monk to the airport. On the drive, little was said; they were both nursing their own memories. When it was time for Monk to board the plane and O'Rourke had walked on ahead a little, Monk turned and embraced Mark, a good warm hug, his eyes soft. "Mark, I knew what it would be like with you. It was more than a hunch. I like knowing you're with me. This can't be a parting, Mark. Be with me, wherever you are."

Deeply touched, Mark again wondered if Monk wished he had had a son. Trying to hide his own feelings, he said, "Oh I'll be with you sooner than you think, Jeremy. Just keep me in mind. I'm with you anyway, but I'll get to Paris as a journalist. It's settled in my mind. I've got to, Jeremy, so I will."

"Oh, you will, Mark. I feel it in my bones. You will," Monk said, as he moved away.

"Save me a chair on the boulevard," Mark called after him, "and remember me to Cretia." Monk waved, then was gone. But not gone for long, Mark told himself, feeling at loose ends as he left the airport.

Winter passed, spring came, and one day in May in the Press Club he read that the internationally celebrated Jeremy Monk had married Cretia in Paris. Their pictures were in the paper. He read the story, stared at the pictures, separate pictures, not taken together. This fascinated him; he couldn't believe the story. For hours he sat in his bedroom in the big house. At midnight, he went for a long walk. It started to rain, a light spring rain that felt good on his bare head and made the wet pavements shine in taxi headlights. He kept hearing voices; he heard Cretia's voice, then Jeremy's, and

Jeremy said, "But Mark, dear boy, you never told me you loved Cretia. She knew you were travelling with me, but she never wrote to you, did she? You never wrote to her. Not once. So how can you believe I just pushed you aside?" But the voice saying these things began to enrage him, and he thought bitterly: All right, all right. But how can you be such a fool, Jeremy? Oh, goddamn you, Jeremy.

When he got home he sat in his kitchen, staying there until late at night with his brandy bottle, getting drunk. Finally, with a strange smile on his face, he slapped the kitchen table hard and said aloud, "Yes, that's right. I don't have to believe in it. Separate pictures! I can't believe it till I really see them together." Then in a stupor, his head dropped to the table, but before he went to sleep he cried, "Besides, Cretia and I have a date to go to Chartres."

Since his father's estate had been settled, he now had an assured income. As the winter passed, he got more assignments from the newspaper. On the first day of spring, through a contact at the Press Club, he was given a chance to go to Vietnam, to Saigon, a job he could have done with bitter relish, but the management of the paper said no. The fact that Americans were paying his expenses would make him their man, or seem to be their man in Vietnam, seeing what they wanted him to see. This was unacceptable. At this time, the editor talked about putting him on the permanent staff. When he didn't jump at the offer they were astonished, but a little later, with the snow gone and the good weather coming on, he met Nancy Holman, over from London — she was the London bureau — and he talked to her about being a Paris correspondent. The paper didn't have a Paris bureau. Miss Holman, a tall good-looking egomaniac with a mouth like Marilyn Monroe's, encouraged him.

"Keep talking to them," she said. "Don't give up on it. It would be nice to visit you in Paris."

"Put in a word for me," he said, and kissed her. A month later, he read a notice in the *New York Times* that Jeremy Monk's new book, *The Galilean*, already released in England, was due for a September publication. That very night, when he came home from the Press Club, he found the mailman had left a package from London — the book, *The Galilean*. Inside on the title page, Monk had written, "As I told you, dear Mark — after the ground had been cleared for me — here I am."

He read on the dust jacket how Jeremy Monk, accompanied by his young bride, had gone to Palestine in search of some fresh view of the Galilean, hoping to find it in the ancient holy places. "What's he up to? What's driving him now?" Mark said aloud. Sitting down, he began to read, then couldn't put the book down, held as he was in spite of himself in the spell of Monk's words, by the authenticity of his imagination and the sheer beauty of his descriptions. Monk had created an ancient Jerusalem so he could look at it and walk away from it; he visited Bethlehem, then the places that had become Christian shrines, and always was dissatisfied, always finding the Galilean hidden. He dwelt on the Essenes and all that had been learned about them from the ancient scrolls. Profoundly discontented, he took his young wife deep into the desert. There, he was stirred, stunned, his imagination inflamed. From then on, he knew the thing he searched for, the illumination, the certainty of its truth, could be found deep in the desert. This striking chapter moved Mark and filled him with wonder: the Jew in the desert, the desert from time immemorial in all Jews, the smell, the strange lights, the sandstorms, the desolate spaces, the death in it, the madness, the visions; and the Galilean Monk sought, he had gone into this desert and taken it deep inside himself. Monk wrote that at times he felt frightened. He could feel the awful desolation of the sand littered with bleak cold rocks seeping into his own being, making him

shiver with cold and loneliness, and yet as this desert
widened in him, he was drawn on and on till finally, filled
first with a strange expectancy, then, in a glowing certainty,
he knew he could find the Galilean only by going deeper
into the desert within himself.

"My God," Mark thought when he got free from the grip
of Monk's words. "Is this Monk? Was he ever a socialist?
What the hell is happening to him? Is it the marriage?"

In a turmoil, he began to pace up and down, struggling
against an overwhelming sense of loss, then growing uneasy,
he stopped his pacing, and full of wonder, thought, Look what
he's doing. As a writer he was one thing, the biggest thing in
my life. He's turned it all around. Just to be with Cretia? He
turned that around, too. He's turned everything around. Now
I don't know what to think. But Monk had sent the book to
him. Why? Did Monk feel they were that close? Did he need to
feel he had a young friend who would follow him all the way?
What's he up to? Mark wondered. Where's he going? Am I
not supposed to see that he's betraying everything his work
stood for? What a letdown! And he stood in a trance, nursing
his disappointment and wonder. But his belief in Monk and his
affection for him had been so deep, he tried to tell himself that
Monk had merely become a Christian socialist. He told himself
Monk had come to believe in the dignity and importance of
the person, and was seeing this as a part of his old quest for a
new and greater freedom.

That night, he wrote a brief note to Monk, addressing it
to the English publisher: "Dear Jeremy, thanks for the book,
a lovely piece of writing. But it upsets me. What are you up
to? Are you to be St Jeremy? I must talk to you. It's very
important to me."

But when he posted the letter he wondered uneasily if he
would ever hear from Monk again.

In the passing weeks, Mark found that others in England
and the United States were equally confused by the change

in Monk's view. Just as he'd called Monk, St Jeremy, so did the reviewer in the London *Sunday Times*. Apparently, everyone in England now knew about Jeremy Monk, and he was sneered at or praised. In the United States, when the book appeared, the celebrated Christian capitalist journalist, Brinkly T. Brooker, Sr., wrote a great tribute on the front page of the *New York Times Book Review*. Fascinated by Monk's view of the desert within, Brinkly T. Brooker, Sr., took this to mean, writing eloquently, that Monk was informing us that life, his life, his socialism, his incursions into Marxism had been this desert, and now, having come through, he had found a new life. The fool. It's not the book I read, Mark thought. One of the few, fresh, thought-provoking minds of our time, the right-wing Brooker wrote.

In late September, when he finally made arrangements with the managing editor for a move to Paris, he couldn't bring himself to write to Monk. He wanted to appear in Paris — suddenly — his arms out to him. He had worked out a very nice arrangement with the paper. They agreed to give him a retainer, and on top of that, pay him space rates for any European story he wrote. He was to be in continual contact with the London bureau who might ask him at any time to cover a Paris story. There was new restlessness in Paris. De Gaulle and his followers had marched in the streets. Josephine Baker had marched with him. But there had been student riots, too. Before leaving home, Mark made arrangements with Joyce to take Alfie to live with her. She promised to keep mentioning him to the dog from time to time, for even if he were away for a year, Alfie would be little more than a pup on his return. Both Joyce and Alfie came to the airport with him. In the late afternoon, when he arrived in Paris, he went directly to the small hotel, the Paris-New-York, down Vaugirard, the longest street in Paris. The hotel had been recommended to him by the London bureau. He had a bedroom, and a small adjoining room he could use for work, all only minutes away from the Deux Magots, and if he wanted to walk, he could quickly get to La Coupole on Montparnasse. Tired out, he lay on the bed and slept until nightfall.

It was like a mid-summer night in Paris, though it was the end of September. That was the way it was in Paris, with April often too cool but a surprising late-September real summer warmth. He walked up Vaugirard to boulevard du Montparnasse, then along the boulevard, just to get the feel of the place, and as he used to do, he went to La Coupole for dinner to see if his favourite waiter was still there and would remember him. He did. Drinking and letting his mind wander, he moved out to the terrace, where he had first met Monk. At midnight, he took a taxi to his hotel and slept till nearly noon. After he had had his lunch, he came back to the hotel, looked up Jethroe's number in the phone book and called him. Jethroe's wife answered. "Mark Didion," he said, his heart beating, as if he knew everything could at that moment go wrong. "Do you remember me?"

"Mark. Jeremy's friend. Of course I remember you," and he heard her calling to her husband, who came to the phone. "I'm here as a journalist now," Mark said. "I knew you'd be able to tell me if Jeremy is in town."

"Jeremy is in London, plugging his book," Jethroe said. "Look here, Mark, I'd like to talk to you about Jeremy. You must know things about him now we'd like to know."

"Then you and your wife have dinner with me," he said.

"No, no, no," Jethroe said. "You come here. Can you come tonight? We insist. Come at eight-thirty. It's easier for us."

He found a flower shop on Montparnasse just below La Closerie and he sent a dozen long-stemmed red roses to Mrs. Jethroe. He found his sense of expectancy growing; it heightened as he waited during the long afternoon. He took an aperitif and waited in La Closerie, only a ten-minute walk from the Jethroe atelier, and he kept looking at his watch.

Jethroe, thin, wiry, grey and with a good colour, came to the door. Behind him, his young wife and the Greek girl with the tantalizing little hook of her nose that drew his eyes to her voluptuous mouth, there as if they hadn't moved, their faces even more attractive because of the unexpected warmth of interest in him. "Tell us about Jeremy, Mark," Mrs. Jethroe said. "What in the world happened to Jeremy on your travels? He's like a bishop now. What did you do to him, Mark? Look," she went on, pointing to the table. "Your flowers. How did you know I loved roses? Sit down, Mark."

He faced the rear of the studio and there, as it had been, the high window with the heavy black shadow at the top, and still there too, against the wall, Jethroe's paintings, the stack Cretia had been looking at when her hand had come out to him.

While Jethroe poured the wine, his wife and the Greek girl, hurrying back and forth from the kitchen, called in turn, "Whatever it was that happened to Jeremy has certainly paid off"; and, "How do you like him as a big celebrity, Mark?" She brought in salads; the Greek girl followed with poached salmon, and said with her charming leer, "There's even a difference in Jeremy's touch. It used to be so beautifully licentious I'd close my eyes. Now I feel I'm getting a papal blessing."

As yet, they hadn't mentioned Jeremy's marriage. All during dinner, he waited for one to say, "Why did he do it? Is it fair to Cretia? . . . But at his age I suppose he couldn't resist. Poor man!" Mark felt he should not be the one to say this; not with the painter there with his own contented young wife. "Jeremy used to be a very private person," Jethroe said, "Neglected, yes, but great. But as a public presence I don't seem to know him."

"I do," Mark said. "Wild old Jeremy. I wonder if he knows how he's turned things around for me, if I believe him. I'm just itching to see him. I've got so much to say, so many questions to ask," and then, embarrassed by his own warmth, he explained: "He talks to me, you know."

He told them about the night in Winnipeg when Jeremy had encountered the two academics who had fought against Franco in the Spanish Civil War, and how they had known all about him in those days, and how they had embraced, old comrades, and how deeply moving it had been, watching and listening to them, so that he couldn't believe Monk now regarded those great days as a spiritual wasteland, a desert. "I'll have to hear him say it to me. Oh, that goddamned desert. Maybe we should take up a collection to keep him out of deserts. Do you believe he really meant what he said, those great early days of his, a wasteland?"

"Well, he wrote what he wrote."

"A metaphor, just a metaphor. Come on now."

"I think he does believe it now, yes, I do," Jethroe said.

"You're kidding."

"A man can believe anything he wants to believe," Jethroe said. "But it's not the question," he added profoundly.

"What's the question?"

"The question is — can he go on?"

"Who's to stop him?"

"Maybe his own temperament, I hope."

"What is this?" Mark said, baffled. Lighting his pipe, the old painter held up the match flame for his wife, sitting so close to him, to blow out, and then he kissed her pursed lips as the Greek girl, too, brushed her face affectionately against him, the always-present sexuality of his women seemingly to delight the old painter. "Each man has his own temperament," he said finally. "Don't ask me why. Do I ask why an egg is an egg and a tomato a tomato? And why a tomato can't be an egg?"

There were things each man could do, he went on, and things he couldn't do without breaking the pattern of his nature. It used to be called destiny, he said. Then, his blue eyes bright and full of wonder, leaning closer to Mark, he said he had been reading about genes — like little silicon chips in us. What is written on these chips we don't know, he said. Well, he had come to believe it was in the genes, and true for each one of us, that we had to have love, maybe had to have wars, and had to have compassion. The great and special singular talents — all written in the genes. Yes, the sense of beauty and truth, oh, yes, it may be put there in the genes. A man's individual true direction is there in his genes. "Well, is Jeremy now trying to break the pattern set for his nature?"

"He is! Of course, he is," Mark said.

"In that case, what will happen to him is out of his hands," Jethroe said, shrugging.

"Jeremy? Out of Jeremy's hands? Oh, no. Not Jeremy," Mark said, grinning.

"Oh, such lofty talk," the Greek said, throwing up her hands. "I don't understand this talk. Anyway, Balzac said it for all."

"Balzac?"

"Yes, Balzac. Oh, to be famous and to be loved. Jeremy is now famous and rich and loved."

"Cretia?"

"Ah, Cretia," Jethroe said.

"How is Cretia?" and Mark said quietly, "Is she happy?"

"Oh, she's still carried away. You should see her."

"I'd love to see her."

"Really? Well, why don't we phone her?" Jethroe said. "You phone her, darling."

"Why not?" his wife said, leaving the table.

Returning in two minutes, she said Cretia, alone in her apartment, reading and thinking of going to bed, would join them for a drink in about fifteen minutes. Waiting, Mark said not a word. Then, when Jethroe opened the door, Cretia came in, looked around, silent, staring at Mark, who had his hands out. She came to him. She was in a blue dress, her shoulders bare. But the mysterious change in her face startled him. Her eyes were a little too bright, too far away, the face he had seen in his dreams was now truly dreamlike, or moonlit in its soft serenity, till she gave him her funny little smile, then her shy grin. "Hello, Mark," she said. Impulsively, he put his arms around her, kissing her lightly on the mouth, the taste of her mouth as he remembered it. She started to cry. The others, startled, then embarrassed, said nothing, but not bothering to touch the tears on her cheeks, she laughed. "I'm always like this when I'm glad to see someone and it's a surprise," she said.

"But I told you I'd be seeing you," Mark said. "We were to go to Chartres, remember?"

"Yes, I was to show you Chartres."

"On your motorcycle?"

"No, I have a little car, now."

"All right. In the little car, tomorrow. That's why I'm here, I think," and he laughed, and they all laughed and Cretia sat down and had a cognac.

She said she had heard from Jeremy that morning. In three days he would be in Paris. Then she talked gaily about the success of *The Galilean*, and about an English bishop who had brought Jeremy up to spend a weekend at his house, and all the other public figures who were seeking Jeremy out. It was a good evening, they seemed to like each other. When Jethroe confessed he was tired and needed sleep they all embraced. Cretia said she would drive Mark to his hotel in her little red car. On the drive, nothing was said. It was as if he knew nothing was needed but silence. At the hotel, she shook his hand. "I'll pick you up at ten right here," she said.

◊ THIRTEEN ◊

S HE CAME INTO THE hotel in the morning, with the same straight free-swinging stride he remembered, so he could believe nothing had changed for them. She had on a black cashmere turtlenecked sweater and a black leather skirt. Driving through Paris streets to the highway, he talked casually about his newspaper work. She was Monk's wife now, but not on this trip, he told himself grimly. The date had been made before she had married Monk — it was his date — and they were on the road keeping the date, driving past autumn fields and trees with falling leaves, and browning farmlands. "It's true that you didn't like Jeremy's book, isn't it?" she asked.

"Like it? I couldn't put it down," he said. "Look, Cretia, I'd like to think now I could be wrong — that I'd meet him and see that I've got him all wrong. I've got to see him, Cretia."

"Oh, you'll see him."

"Maybe I don't count with him now, Cretia."

"I think from the beginning you touched something in him. You were young. You knew his work so well. You made him feel young. You made him feel he'd remain young in his work wherever it took him."

"It took him to the desert."

"And I was there with him, Mark. It's a true book, a good book."

"It's a most remarkable book — as a piece of writing — but coming from Jeremy Monk — come on, Cretia! And what's next from him? Where's he going now?"

"I don't know. Nor does he."

"I'm sure he does," he said drily.

"Oh, Mark. Why be so cynical?" she said gently, and though never taking her eyes off the road, she rested her head against his shoulder for a moment, brushing her hair against his cheek. "Do you know Baudelaire?"

"*Notre* Baudelaire," he said.

"What?"

"At graduate school, there were two young Jews who had converted to Christianity, after living here in Paris in the neo-Thomistic movement. One was from New York, the other from Chicago. After a holiday, when they met, clasping hands, one would say, '*Notre* Baudelaire,' and the other '*Notre* Baudelaire.' Now you. Why Baudelaire?"

"Remember his old captain on the prow of his ship sailing on, forever seeking something new?"

"Sure."

"That's Jeremy."

"Jeremy, our old mariner. The ancient mariner. I'm joking, Cretia. It's okay. Since you know all about great mystical voyages, how come I was so sure I'd see Chartres with you?"

"Well, it was a date, wasn't it?"

"A date with a stranger. I was a stranger."

"No, you weren't. No one had to tell me anything about you."

"Come to think of it," he said, "I never asked Jeremy to tell me things about you. I had what you gave me and I thought Jeremy couldn't tell me anything I really wanted to know. I was wrong. I didn't want to know he knew you would marry him. You see, you were always in my mind, telling me other things."

"Secret things?" she asked, smiling. "And you listened?"

"At night in my bed I listened. But now that you're married, and you're still in my mind . . ."

"Still telling you things?"

"All kinds of things, yet never with me now . . ."

"Oh, we'll meet and part, and meet again," she said softly. He couldn't fathom the expression on her face. His eyes went to her ankle above the gas pedal, to her calf, to the hem of the black leather skirt above her knee. Monk's wife. Monk — old enough to be her father! Catching his breath, he wondered what in hell he imagined could happen in Chartres and why was it so very important that they get to Chartres so he could see her against the great high blue window. Passing through the next village, she said they could make a turn and go to Versailles and he could walk where kings had walked. Another time, he said. There would have to be another time, and he had a fear now of touching her. He started talking about Monk in western Canada, a giant on the road, and he was only a disciple, a moment among wild horses lost in the snow, the swirl of snow. She talked about the hill towns of Assisi. It was as if they were afraid of a silence; all their words were a garbled translation of some language of the body which was clear if they remained silent. At a village twenty miles from Chartres, they had lunch and a carafe of red wine. The innkeeper, a jolly short man with a long moustache and a thin weary wife, gave them two roses, the last of the summer roses. Just for them, he said with a knowing smile. They drove on to Chartres, a bustling old town of too much greyness, Mark thought, old and grey, but always a presence as long as the cathedral stood in the wide square. There were not many people in the square. Four American women, shivering in sundresses, three beefy men wearing Bavarian hats who carried cameras. To the left of the square, a small fair with games of chance, a shooting gallery and a fast-food kiosk, out of season now.

Taking her hand, he asked, "Who was it that said Chartres is all of France?"

"It must have been an American," she said. "It doesn't sound like a Frenchman."

"It's always the Americans who know these things," he said. "And see that building over there to the left? The wing of the building with those windows? That must be the hotel where James Baldwin stayed, and he looked at the cathedral and wrote that endless hours, endless years of forced labour went into the building of the church just to satisfy some bishop's craving for glory."

"Ah, such fellow citizens you have, Mark."

"I don't know the man."

"Did he go into the cathedral?"

"Come to think of it, he didn't say so."

"Such a damn fool bookkeeper. Come on," she said giving him an impatient tug for he had been made mute and motionless by the harmony of proportion in the old church, a harmony mirroring some longing for perfection in people who had lived around the grey church eight hundred years ago. Yet, it was not as massive as Notre Dame or Rheims, it had nothing of the late flamboyant Gothic; it was of an earlier harmony of proportion, a lightness of form, reflecting the inner world of a life once lived here.

"Mark! Come on," she said again. As they crossed the square, she wrapped a handkerchief over her head. Opening the church door, he was counting on the satisfaction of seeing her face against the high blue window behind the altar. He let her go a little ahead so she would have to turn, waiting. She turned. The shape of her face changed slightly in that blue light, yet it was just as he imagined, a face finding its time in that window, a Florentine face, a Roman face, a face from the troubadour country. Moving to the right, she knelt in a pew, bowing her head in prayer. He waited, eyes on the handkerchief wrapped around her head, surprised she could be so rapt in prayer. He moved ahead, absorbed, wondering. Then, turning to the left, examining the wood carvings and the other stained-glass windows, he imagined the sculptured heads of the apostles all around were watching him. The apostles had the faces of plain homely men, who might have come in to pose from nearby streets, and they knew he was a stranger in their neighbourhood. He had counted on Cretia being there beside him, her face full of that elation she had shown while looking at Monet's garden paintings. Something was spoiled for him, something lost. Disappointed, he went back down the aisle to the pew where she still prayed. "Cretia," he said, then felt foolish, for in her devotion she looked as her face had told him she would look.

"Yes," she said turning.

"I didn't know you were so devout."

"It's in the family; my uncle is a bishop and a theologian, don't you remember?"

"The thing is, I didn't seem to know you, lost in prayer."

"You've never seen me praying."

"Could I ask what you were praying for?"

"Nothing. Nothing at all. Just letting myself be, a sense that life may be elsewhere."

"Elsewhere?" he repeated. Walking her slowly to the door, he said, "That doesn't sound like you, Cretia. Is that Jeremy? Some of his dust from the desert, strange lights on the sands?" At the open door, she took the handkerchief from her head and with the sunlight on her face, gripped his arm impulsively in a sudden need to draw him close, his arm pressed hard against the curve of her hip as she looked at him with her wise little grin. Then, the leap of expectation mounting in him touched everything — the dim light shed by the church, the trees across the square, the coloured rooftops in light and shadow — with a lovely sensual warmth. "Glory to God for dappled things, Cretia," he said. "I can say that when I'm with you. It's even in the warmth of your hand. Don't let him change you, Cretia."

"Who?"

"Jeremy."

"What am I? A little child? You're funny, really funny."

As they left the square, he could feel her drawing away, then, her mood changing, coming nearer to him.

They had dinner in a hotel. They talked about her father, an industrialist whose impoverished patrician family had owned vineyards and a rambling estate that was run down. He had put his money into the compact-automobile business and had become wealthy, again, and he dreamt of buying back the ancient family acres. He lived in Parioli, a district Jeremy called Mussolini's Rome because it had been developed in the dictator's time. She seemed eager to laugh at her own stories. Sometimes, she talked too brightly. Something else was in the air. Something pushing her one way, and pulling him another.

"I know what's in your mind, Mark," she said suddenly. "And you're wrong. I'm quite happy in my marriage."

"Why not?" he asked, shrugging. "I'm sure Jeremy is a wonderful lover."

"Oh, he was. A wonderful lover."

"Was?"

"Well, now it's another kind of happiness."

"Now . . ."

"Now we have a spiritual marriage. Do you know what that is?"

"A spiritual marriage?" Shocked, wanting to laugh, he was stilled by her serene expression. "Spiritual marriages? Are there such things, Cretia?"

"Oh yes, when there's enough love. . . . A real union beyond any sexual satisfaction. It's another kind of happiness."

"Cretia . . . could I ask? Do you sleep together?"

"Of course we do."

"Lying in bed beside you. Not touching you. Cretia . . ."

Then, with a pitying pang, he remembered her coming into Jethroe's place and he thought he understood the impulsive kiss, her surge of emotion, and in spite of herself, the tears. Moved, he put his hand on hers; with his warm comforting hand on her yielding fingers, she frowned, yet didn't withdraw. In the silence that fell between them, he thought he could see what had happened, he imagined Monk, the experienced lover, confident and strong in the first days of their marriage, loving and exhausting her with his proud virility, and then one night in the dark, when she was naked on the bed, waiting, he got into bed. She opened her arms and, maybe, taking her in his arms, he couldn't take her. He grew frightened as he lay beside her, the chill of death in him, taking his hand from her shoulder, the hand grown cold. His legs would have grown cold, too, his age catching up to him, afraid to ask his young wife to arouse him, afraid to crawl naked out of bed, and growing frantic, lying silent in the dark, while Cretia waited, wondering. But Jeremy's imagination saved him, Mark thought. Whispering, telling her about another kind of love, another kind of ecstasy that could come from denial, he would say, they should try it tonight, and see if there were strange dreams and raptures and visions in these denials. Ghandi took young women into his bed to test the rapture and power in a denial of warm flesh.

"Ah, yes, Cretia," Mark said, stroking her hand, "St Jeremy indeed, and for you — as you said, life must be elsewhere."

"You're here Mark." She grinned. "And I'll always like you."

"Cretia and her strange happiness," he went on, half to himself. "Well, come on, let's go."

"Yes, we must go, we really must," she said. Her eyes were on her hand as it slipped from under his.

"Love in Chartres," she said smiling.

"Let us count the ways," he said as they stood up. "Well, when do I see Jeremy?"

"He'll be home tomorrow."

"Tell him, Mrs. Jeremy Monk, that I must see him. I've been waiting. Tell him I'd like to come around and see your place."

"Yes, Mr. Mark Didion, I certainly will," she said.

Outside, the light had changed to the still hour of dusk, the sky clear and cloudless, and overhead, a pale hunter's moon.

◊ FOURTEEN ◊

THAT NIGHT, MONK RE-turned to Paris and the next day Mark, staying in his hotel, waited to hear from him. He thought he would get a call at about noon. No call came. He stayed around all afternoon, believing Monk would ask him to have dinner in their apartment. Then he would see them together. He would see Cretia with Monk in their home. Even if they asked him to have dinner in a res-taurant, he would see them at last together and might have to believe in their marriage. When the afternoon passed and neither one of them called, he didn't know whether to blame Cretia or Monk. Then he wondered if he would ever see them together. At loose ends, passing the time, he got a postcard and addressed it to Miss Matulak, the taxi driver in Vancouver. He wrote: "Here in Paris. Your friend, Mark." He knew it would delight her.

It was just as well that he hung around the hotel; he got a call from the London bureau. The tall woman, Nancy Hol-man, whose attractive mouth he remembered, and who was his boss now, wanted him to write a human-interest story about the new Paris mayor who had wide communist sup-port. Nancy Holman, a firm woman, said the story should be: Was he a Marxist himself? Did he have ambitions on a national scale? Did he dissociate himself from radical violence? What did he read and what did he like doing in his spare time? The story should be written with a light touch, she said. The London bureau had contacted the mayor's office and they had agreed to give him a half-hour. All this, he thought, would take his mind off Jeremy Monk. But when he was leaving the hotel on his way to the city hall, he told the desk clerk he was expecting a call from a Mr. Monk, who should be told that he would be back in his room by six o'clock. In twenty minutes he was at the Hôtel de Ville.

The mayor, a short plump man with carefully combed, thinning black hair, took a slightly weary condescending air with him, and implied Mark, being from North America, could have no real knowledge of international affairs. "*C'est une question perpétuelle Fenimore Cooper.*" Of course, he said, he was not a Marxist himself, he was a Frenchman; he had the logical mind of a Frenchman. He smiled indulgently, raising his eyebrows when Mark asked him about Jean-Paul Sartre and the communists. He shrugged helplessly. The communists, he said, and this was something the American would never be able to understand, were not necessarily Marxists. "As for Monsieur Sartre and these café considerations . . ." It was obvious that he had never read Sartre and was nettled by Mark's awareness of it. He said spitefully, but with a jolly air, "That's a Québec accent. No? A delightful, rustic flavour to it. *Très fort.* I like it." When Mark asked if he thought the Americans had learned anything from the French defeat in Vietnam, he said, "Of course not. Nothing whatever. Nothing at all," and then, his eye flickering, he realized that Mark was amused, that Mark was simply drawing him out, and he terminated the interview. As they parted, there was more respect in his handshake; it was proper and resolute and he even laughed when Mark said, "As they used to say, and may it always be said, 'France is full of Frenchmen'."

Leaving the office, he came out into the broad great square in front of the Hôtel de Ville, into the unseasonably warm sunlight Paris would have enjoyed in the spring. Just ahead in the square, but a full hundred feet ahead, was a white-haired man in a brown jacket, grey slacks, and hatless. His head, with the crown of white hair, looked all the more remarkable because of his youthful stride. Stopping in astonishment, Mark whistled: a good sharp piercing whistle. The man half turned; then dashed to the taxi stand further along, past a kiosk at the street curb. "Jeremy," Mark yelled. He wanted to tell him he had found *The Galilean* upsetting, and have a warm friendly talk. Calling out again, he started to run, thinking: Jeremy turned, he looked, and kept going but that's all right. I'd be the last person he'd expect to see here. Monk had got into a taxi, and as it pulled away, Mark thought he saw him turn and look back to where he stood at the curb, waving. When another taxi came along, Mark told the driver to follow Monk's cab, which seemed to be heading for the river; it went on past Notre Dame, then crossing the bridge, up the boul' Mich, where it seemed to speed up and get further ahead, almost out of sight, and then at the iron gate to the Luxembourg, it stopped. It was turning slowly. The passenger was gone. Mark lost time paying his driver, then, striding through the gate, he thought he saw Monk far down the path, not hurrying now, not compelled to look back. He got beyond the pond, to the place where children ride the ponies, and he still hadn't looked back. Hurrying by men who were playing *boules*, he gained ground, then was suddenly held up, his attention distracted by a loud altercation near the women's toilet. A well-dressed American girl was being pursued by an angry jabbering crone who spun around her, trying to block her way. The frightened woman called out desperately, "Steve," to a young man waiting twenty feet away. Rushing at the raging lavatory attendant, the young man cried, "*Elle ne parle pas français*," and pulling a fistful of centimes and francs out of his pocket, he shoved them into the elderly attendant's hand. In a sudden magical transformation, the attendant smiled warmly, bowing from the waist. While Mark had been watching, Monk had vanished.

Breaking into a trot, he reached the gate, looked down Vaugirard, then beyond to the next cross street and saw that Monk was close to Raspail, which meant he would turn down toward the Lutétia. But there was a street on this side of Raspail that took a curve toward rue de Babylone and the hotel, eliminating the Raspail corner, and Mark hurried until, not twenty feet from the Lutétia, there was Monk coming toward him. He stopped with an air of surprise. "Mark . . . yes, I heard you were in Paris."

At the sound of his voice, all Mark's old warm affectionate fascination welled up in him, and laughing, his arms wide open, he hugged him warmly. "Ah, Jeremy," he said. "It's good to see you," and he hugged him again; then realizing Monk was not hugging him, he drew back, discomfited, fumbling for words, and said awkwardly, "Well, here we are. Let's have a drink. There's the Lutétia. Remember how you stood there on the steps? The wild old man on the road?"

Hardly smiling, Monk said awkwardly, "I'm in a frightful hurry, Mark. I'm visiting some people with Cretia. I'm late, very late. She'll be wondering what happened to me. I know where you are staying. I intended to call you. I've been tied up. I'm going to the States." After pausing, he added importantly, "A lecture at Harvard, you know. Well, nice seeing you," and he hurried away. Aghast, Mark knew that Monk would not call him. Humiliated, he walked rapidly toward rue du Bac, but then as he slowed down, the hurt in him deepening, he thought, He's dropped me. He doesn't want to have me around.

M ONK WENT TO WASH-
ington and appeared at
a National Press Club luncheon with Brinkly T. Brooker, Sr.,
his Harvard admirer, in a television dialogue that drew a
great deal of attention. Well-known columnists, bemused at
first, then enchanted, listened to the two cultivated intelligent men engaging in a gently intimate meeting of sympathetic minds, talking about their world and — of all things
— God and the Galilean, the desert, the religious experience, Freud, the communists, and the grandeur of
Solzhenitsyn. Brinkly T. Brooker, Sr., an unassailable reac-
tionary conservative with an unruffled sweetly reasonable
manner, who was not only rich but could write well himself,
was full of scholarly insights. The two men, apparently
forgetting that cynical hardboiled newspapermen were
listening, talked as if they were alone, smiling and nodding,
leaning back to reflect, and they stroked each other with
quotations from Aristotle, Thomas Aquinas, John of the
Cross or Bonhoeffer — as if these men lived down their
street. For the cynical pressmen, the dialogue had the charm
of novelty. Monk spoke of the puerility of nakedness as a
political act and sex as "the dreadful necessity" — wondering
if the urge could be sublimated and directed toward God
and thus made more than a clanking chain. Brooker, who
had three children, tapping his teeth with his pencil, looked
grave. Monk said softly that after he had written *The*

Galilean, he knew he was on the way home, he knew that all life was a longing for home. He had learned this in the desert, seeking the Galilean. Then quietly, with a gentle smile, he added, "You know, Brinkly, sometimes I feel so very close to God. It's a strange feeling. An illumination. Closer and closer to God — as if now I only need to go deep into the desert, deeper into the desert."

The overwhelmed luncheon audience gave Monk and Brinkly T. Brooker, Sr., a good hand. The story went out over the wire services. It appeared in the *International Herald Tribune*, and Mark read the story, standing at the counter at Fauchon, having an espresso and a strawberry torte. He was on his way to American Express, on rue Scribe, to see if there was any mail from Joyce, who was still looking after his dog. Monk's astonishing announcement that he was getting closer and closer to God made Mark laugh. He sure knows how to steal the show, he thought. Folding the paper, he stuck it in his side pocket, left Fauchon, and went on his way. He reached the place de l'Opéra and then, as if startled, he stopped dead on the street. It was as if some notion nagging at his memory ever since he had read the paper had broken through, and now came as a flash of insight, an illumination about Monk that excited his imagination and held him there transfixed. Out of some old reading, or conversation, he remembered a Benedictine saying — was it Benedictine or Dominican? — a saying about the Galilean: ". . .in whose service there is perfect freedom." There it was! He remembered the piece Monk had written in the *London Observer*: "A new freedom. Where do I go to find it?" Then, his book on the Galilean. And now, as he said, getting closer to God — to the perfect freedom in Him. "Well, well, it all adds up," Mark said aloud, startling a man who was staring at ties in a shop window and, pleased with himself, he went on to the American Express Company, and there at the counter was Jethroe's wife, looking for letters not addressed to her home. She opened a pale-blue envelope and began to read. She had on a wine-coloured short skirt, the hem three inches above her knees. So lovely with that hair, Mark thought, but no woman should wear a skirt three inches above her knees. No beautiful woman has beautiful knees, not even Cretia with her lovely legs. Seeing him, almost furtively, she put the letter in her purse. As they talked, she asked if he had seen the news about Monk in Washington. "What's he up to this time?" she asked cynically. "Not another book about the desert?"

"Of course," he said. "Now there's always got to be a new book." He asked if he couldn't take her and Jethroe to La Closerie des Lilas and, apparently as a happy afterthought, he asked if she wouldn't like to bring Cretia with her.

Two nights later, Jethroe, his wife and Cretia came in to La Closerie, Cretia in a yellow dress and high heels, and with only a formal kiss for him. The restaurant seemed to be a place where solid, middle-aged, carefully groomed bourgeois Frenchmen and cultural entrepreneurs dined with pretty young expensive girls, obviously not their wives. "My father used to play billiards in La Closerie," Mark said.

"So did I," Jethroe added.

"I'm good at pool and billiards," Cretia said. "I think I could beat you, Mark."

"Not a chance. I'm a shark," he said. "I put myself through college in poolhalls."

When they had ordered, Mark asked, "Have you heard from Jeremy since his appearance at the Press Club in Washington?"

"I have," Cretia said. "You think he says strange things now, don't you?"

"Oh no. I think I've got the hang of him now."

"Good for you," Jethroe said. "Wish I could say the same.

But it's strange to me, this sort of thing coming from my old Republican pal."

"Isn't this incredible?" Cretia asked sweetly. "One of your friends says he believes in God and you go gaw-gaw like something's wrong. Well, you know what's really strange? Those tough-minded men, hearing things they never expected to hear, were strangely attentive and maybe a little embarrassed by their own interest. These men, they know everything from the outside, their own world. And Jeremy was talking about the inside. He knows that everything that really matters, or hurts us, comes from inside where those pressmen never go." Smiling brightly, she lifted her glass of white wine. "And here's a toast to Jeremy's Harvard lecture."

Taken aback, Mark, and then Jethroe and his wife, raised their glasses. "Good girl," Jethroe said. "Wonderful," Mark said, but wondered why her eyes were holding his. They dropped to his hand on the table, and as he shifted it, her eyes followed the movement of his fingers clutching the napkin, and he thought of Chartres, his hand on hers in Chartres. He looked up only when Mrs. Jethroe asked Cretia to go downstairs to the toilet with her.

Jethroe was irritated. "I wanted to ask Cretia something," he said, "but that damned ardent tone put me off. Jeremy said he was on the way home. Where is home, I'd like to know?"

"Have you thought of Rome?"

"Rome? Well! Well! Still, I've often thought how easy it is for a man of the extreme left to become a man of the extreme right. The trouble with Jeremy, as I see it," Jethroe said as Cretia and Mrs. Jethroe came upstairs, "is that he was an idealist, and in every idealist there's a tyrant."

After that, the evening went warmly and easily, as if they were in the Jethroe atelier. As he talked, the old painter kept putting his hand on his young wife's leg. They were among the last to leave the restaurant, long after the old pianist who played by the front door had gone home. The solid middle-aged Frenchmen with their conservative grey suits and their pretty young girls had all gone. They themselves left only because Madame began to grunt and hum beside the cash register and Jethroe's back was beginning to bother him, a little cramp, then a severe one that cut off his breath just as he was talking eloquently about Miró, the dapper little painter whom he had known before the days of Miró's public greatness. The Jethroes said they would walk the few blocks home. Alone in the car with Cretia, Mark said, "I'd like to see where you live."

"I live about five minutes walk from St Sulpice. You've heard of St Sulpice art? The sentimentalizing."

"To St Sulpice then. Show me your place Cretia."

"Why not?" she said.

"Ah, that sounds like Cretia."

"I always sound like Cretia," she said, and they drove down Montparnasse, turning at Raspail, past Rodin's great *Balzac* brooding over the corner, and within a few minutes they were at an old stone building, an apartment house with a heavy oak door, a shadowy vestibule and an iron gate to a courtyard garden. She led him upstairs to an apartment with a wide hall and high ceilings. A Siamese cat came wandering along the hall to brush against her. The apartment was furnished with Louis XVI furniture, the right apartment for a public figure with a beautiful young wife, and yet, as Mark saw, looking around in surprise, the walls were bare but for a mirror here, a mirror there, mirrors in severe pewter frames. "How strange," he said. "Not a painting, yet you're a painter. All this austerity! Not a splash of colour. This isn't you Cretia. It isn't Jeremy. Jeremy, the most sensual of men. He used to love the glory of colour."

"Better bare walls than something you no longer like," she said defensively. "Anyway, we haven't had time to put up paintings."

"Where do you work? I'd love to see something."

"Oh, you will, sometime."

"Aren't you painting now?"

"I'll start painting again, Mark. I know I will," and she looked around, troubled. "I don't know. Maybe I feel these walls don't seem ready for anything I might do. I'll have to see. Look, you say you're a pool shark."

"I am."

"I know I can beat you. We'll go to La Closerie, won't we?"

"It's a deal," he said, and stretching out on the long deep grey couch, he watched her go to the inlaid cabinet where the cognac and glasses were. Her back was to him; he could see the little tufts of hair at the back of her long neck, the hair he had nestled in as he rode behind her on her motorbike. The hem of her yellow dress fell just below her knees. The Siamese, purring loudly, brushed against her calf. The cat's purring and her high heels made him catch his breath.

"Cretia," he said, "I love you a lot, you know."

"What?"

"I love you."

"Do you, Mark?" she said without turning.

"I know I'm here in Jeremy's house."

"Yes, and I'm Jeremy's wife," she said, facing him.

"You're not his wife now. Come on, Cretia. It's not a real marriage now."

"Isn't it? When he's always close beside me? In some ways, even closer now. Isn't that a marriage?"

"You and I are closer now," he said, and he stood up. "If you could feel the way my heart is beating — oh, hell, Cretia. You shouldn't let him do this — change your nature the way he is changing his — It's all wrong," he protested. "It's against life. It's against your whole warm nature." She moved away from the little elegant cabinet, her back turned to him as she sipped her brandy, his eyes on the little tuft of neck hair. In his dreams he had kept seeing a tuft, and he said, "You know what I think Cretia?"

"I know. . . . Indeed I do."

"No, you don't. It's his age," he said brutally.

"Mark, don't. That's cheap. It's banal."

"No, there's a time, Cretia. There comes a time for a man his age who has loved a hundred women when his body suddenly fails him. There comes a time. A horror. And you, in the dark, beside him always waiting." Faltering, the hurt in her eyes shaming him, he grew angry, yet he couldn't stop. "What can he do? Is it a sign? My God, he takes it as a sign. A lover now of spiritual things, impotence as a sign, he thinks his body is telling him something, he imagines a new way to love. To keep you beside him. Oh, shit, Cretia!" and he got up from the couch, staring at her angrily as she brushed at her yellow dress, her cheeks flushing.

"Shit on you," she said trembling. "You think it's outrageous. Sure, it's a new experience for me. But I know Jeremy loves me, maybe more than ever now. I mean he seems to need me more than ever. And at night, lying beside him, as he said I would, I experience strange ecstasies in denial. It's like . . . like the denial sharpens all my senses; it even inflames my imagination. My dreams, my fantasies now are all in high bright warm colours, my body light and so warm, and back in my mind is the memory of his lovemaking. Oh, how he could love! A kind of fragrance grew from our bodies. I remember, yes, I remember. Yes, then I believe that in spite of his denial he is secretly waiting, lying beside me, waiting — as I am waiting, yes, like waiting for him to come home. Oh, yes."

Her eyes were filled with tears. He watched the slow rise and fall of her breathing, her parted lips and her half-closed eyes. "Like waiting for him to come home, yes," she whispered. "But waiting, it gets so goddamned lonely." While she said these things, the flush on her cheeks told him something else; her eyes, reaching for him, said something else; and so too her body, excited by her own words, and the cat was brushing against her calf softly in its rhythmic purring. He took her in his arms and kissed her. Startled, her eyes blank, her body stiffened against him. "Mark, no," she cried. She held his hands as they went over her body, then she gripped them. Yet her hands moved with his hands as he drew her to the couch. He heard her low wild moan of protest. He pulled the yellow dress from one shoulder, then off the other till her breasts were bare. He lay on her. Her nipple was in his mouth. But her body lay inert between his knees. Raising his head a little, he saw that her eyes were closed, her mouth twisted in anguish, and tears were streaming down her cheeks. "Cretia," he said. "My God, Cretia. No, no." As he uttered his own desolate cry, his whole body went inert, his erection, too. Confused, nervous, he tightened up, wondering if the sudden loss of lust could be from the pain he felt at Cretia's tears, or if both of them felt that Jeremy, in his own house, was watching them.

"What is it? What is this?" Then he said gently, "Take it easy, Cretia. Take it easy," and with his handkerchief he dried her eyes. Helping her up, he tried to straighten her dress. "It's — I don't know — it's me," he said, worrying. "I love you very much."

"It's all right, Mark," she said. "I don't understand. Neither do you."

The Siamese cat, thrown off the couch, was lying on the rug; it got up, stretched, jumped, and lay beside Cretia, who now sat motionless, her thoughts far away. The strange stillness in her fascinated him. Her fingers went out to the cat, fingers going lightly through the fur, then into her stillness came as sweet and serene an expression as he had ever seen on a woman's face, and it broke his heart.

◊ SIXTEEN ◊

THAT NIGHT HE HAD A dream, and in the dream, leaving Cretia's apartment, he stood with her in the hall. "I should have pulled your clothes off and taken you," he said, and she said, "Why didn't you?" Then, wide awake, he could still hear her dream whisper. "Why didn't you?" and he couldn't sleep; he kept muttering, "Why aren't I like myself. Why am I like someone watching detached?"

In the morning he got a call from Nancy Holman in London, who had a suggestion for a story. In London, they had learned that Ashley Crippen of the British Foreign Office, a close friend of Wilfrid Staley, who was formerly of the Foreign Office until he defected and fled to Moscow, was living in Bayonne on the Spanish border. British intelligence had discovered that Crippen had secretly been a member of the communist party. They had, as yet, no proof that he was a Russian agent, but Staley was his beloved friend. Crippen hadn't waited for them to question him. He had fled and was living in some comfort in Bayonne, close to the casino in Biarritz.

Talking on the phone to Cretia, he told her he would be gone for two or three days and she should find a pool table and practise, and as for him, he would be thinking of her when the train got to the Pyrenees. The train did not go that far. It went through Bordeaux, down along the coast. He had time on the train, wondering what had blocked his possession of Cretia. Then he told himself it couldn't have been otherwise; they had been in Monk's home.

Getting to Bayonne late in the afternoon, he found Ashley Crippen was indeed registered at the hotel, but the desk clerk said Mr. Crippen had gone across the border to San Sebastin for the bullfights. However, Mr. Crippen had said he would be back by noon the next day. After getting a room at the hotel, Mark wandered in the old Basque town, trying to get his mind off Cretia and Monk's strange and moving hold on her. Or, maybe, she was home to Monk. The secret private home for the public man. I'm a fool, he thought. Now I'm letting Monk take me over, too. To get away from brooding, he took a taxi to Biarritz and had dinner at one of the grand hotels. After dinner, he tried to get into the casino; he wasn't in evening dress, they said, so he drank three brandies at a little café facing the beach, and got so very sleepy listening to the sound of the surf, breaking white in the light from the moon and the cafés, that he was hardly able to stay awake in the taxi on the way back to the hotel. Then he slept; he slept very late.

At noontime, he met Ashley Crippen, a roly-poly little fat man who, at lunch with him, confessed he was delighted to be visited by a correspondent. Here, in the Basque country, he led a wonderful life playing tennis and gambling, but sometimes he felt cut off from the great world. He was a homosexual and proud of it, and proud too, he said of his friends, and his stories; with bright witty malice he talked about Noel Coward, Evelyn Waugh and Randolph Churchill. He's on top of them all, Mark thought, always on top! Celebrity! — the world Ashley really wanted, the spiritual state in our time.

That evening, they went to Biarritz, had dinner, and while drinking by the seaside, the roll of the sea got Crippen talking about his life in a lighthearted flip giddy way. Everything had gone his way. He had been to a public school and to

Cambridge; a job had been found for old Ashley, yet he had secretly joined the communist party. He frowned, trying to outdrink Mark. It became plain that Crippen had secretly hated the forces in England that had produced him.

"It's a giddy country," he said. "The rich get richer and the poor get poorer, all of us cemented, so to speak, by our wonderful caste system, in which there is a paradise, a purgatory and a hell, and well, there you are. Those who are in hell never get out, those in purgatory may well slip back to hell, and a chosen few slip up into paradise, but those in hell are there forever. Beastly. Just think, Mr. Didion, all my life I've been in a place that is paradise, yet here I am, all alone by that wide sea out there." But by God, he said, he was still an Englishman, and he had no objection at all if Mark portrayed him as an eccentric Englishman who dreamed of seeing Moscow before he died. "But not yet, oh Lord, not yet. It's too soon," and he grinned. Though he was in limbo, waiting, he wanted some more public attention.

Next day, when they were in the hotel lobby, Crippen suggested they go to Lourdes. "Let's go see some miracles," he said. Then a young man came in, a slim young man with big soft brown eyes, and he looked shyly at Crippen. There was some sign of recognition, some signal, though nothing was said, and Crippen quickly joined the young man and they left the hotel. Hurrying to his room, Mark called the desk, found that he could catch a train to Paris within an hour, then asked the switchboard operator to put through a call to Cretia's apartment in Paris. Ten minutes later he heard Cretia saying, "Mark, is it you?" After telling her he had the story he wanted, he asked, "Tell me something, Cretia. Do the words, 'Why didn't you?' mean anything to you?" Surprised, she said, "No, no. What is this about?" "In a dream, I heard it," he said. "Could it have been your voice I heard in the dream?" Her long silence seemed to tell him something. Finally she said, "I'm baffled. What is this?"

Laughing, he told her he'd like to meet her at La Closerie des Lilas at ten that evening and then they would go somewhere to shoot a little pool, as planned. "Oh, I'd like that," she said, sounding exhilarated.

On the train, he worked on his story about Ashley Crippen and by the time he got to Paris he had finished a rough draft. It was about half-past nine when he arrived. It was a surprisingly chilly evening. He took a taxi to his hotel and then to La Closerie des Lilas. When he got to the café, he found Cretia sitting at the bar wearing a white sweater-coat, rose-coloured slacks, an old-fashioned inch-deep silver necklace and high heels. Her kiss was on his mouth. He talked about his sinister lighthearted fugitive from the British Foreign Office. "Just a minute," she said. "Those words you asked me about, remember? A woman in a dream saying, 'Why didn't you?' No wonder you remembered such a dream. Look, if I walked around this café whispering, 'Why didn't you?' to each one of these people, well, naturally, they'd feel baffled at first, then they'd feel guilty. But what did your dream woman look like? It was a woman, wasn't it?"

"I couldn't tell," Mark said, and she repeated softly to herself. "Why didn't you? Why didn't you; isn't it fascinating? I remember when I was sixteen in Rome. A man about thirty was in love with me. He made movies. But something went wrong. His director walked out on him; it all ended badly; he was in tears, and he said 'It was all about money. I thought of asking you to borrow the money from your father. It would have saved me.' 'Why didn't you?' I said to him. 'Why didn't you?' Absorbed in his failure he would go on, 'If only . . . if only . . .' Well, I got tired of it and broke off with him. I was sure my 'Why didn't you?' and his 'If only' would always be there to make me sad."

Taking her hand, Mark said, "If only — if only," and looking at her palm, he rubbed it against his cheek. After a moment she said, "It's a long time since they had pool tables here."

"It's too bad," he said. "My father played here. In his diary he talked about the sound of the violins coming from under the chestnut trees here while he played billiards."

"Well, the chestnut trees are gone — look around. And so is your father," she said. "But I think I know another place. It's not far away. I think it's over by the Gare Montparnasse."

She knew about this place, she said, because one night when she was in a restaurant called Aux Îles Marquises, Sam Becket was there, and she was told that whenever he came there he played billiards in the café on the rue de la Gaîté, not far from the restaurant. "So let's get in my car," she said. "Come on." They drove to the rue de la Gaîté, and driving slowly along the street they searched for the café, passing four theatres in a neighbourhood of sex shops and brothels and not much else. Finally, Mark got out of the car at a café and asked a waiter where he could play billiards. "Just around the corner," the waiter said, and there indeed, just around the corner, opposite the entrance to the Montparnasse station, was the fine clear airy place — the waiters all traditional — with lots of games: pinball machines, slot machines and the billiard tables.

As soon as she picked up her cue, her manner changed; the face he thought belonged to the blue window of Chartres appeared under the cone of light as she bent over the green baize, her body and arms moving with an easy assurance, and he thought of her motorbike, and the way she walked.

"Where did you learn the game?" he asked. "My father," she said. Later, he said, "Your father must have been a pool hustler." He couldn't beat her, and he liked her proud little swagger.

"Now, back to La Closerie for a drink; a place where we can feel at home," he said. As soon as they had entered the bar at La Closerie, Heffernan, who was sitting by himself at the bar, saw them. He watched, waiting for them to sit down, then picking up his drink, joined them at their table. "Bless you, bless you both. I was getting lonely," he said.

The biographer of Jeremy Monk was looking very neat and very Oxonian in a tweed jacket and grey slacks. He had a folded newspaper in his pocket. As he let Mark buy him a drink, he explained that he had just come from London. He had come to see Jeremy who, he understood, would be in Paris in two days. "I called your apartment," he said to Cretia. "I thought you might want to see this. Look." Taking the *Sunday Telegraph* from his pocket, he spread the page out on the table so they could both see the large photograph of Jeremy Monk.

The picture was taken, as the cutline said, when Monk was delivering his Harvard lecture. There he was, very erect, the shock of hair a crown, the face more than ever an ancient compelling skull, the open mouth suggesting words were coming out of some deep primal wisdom. His right hand, raised to his shoulder, was about to be drawn slowly across his body. An actor's gesture! Mark thought. The whole posture of austere and ancient dignity.

They read the story; Cretia, her head close to his, her breath on his cheek, saying nothing as she read. The headline read, "Monk at Harvard says American withdrawal from Vietnam would be an act of shameful cowardice." In the speech, Monk said that those men, women and students marching in the streets, calling for an end to the war, had lost all moral fibre. They advocated surrender — not just to the North Vietnamese, but to the sinister evil force behind that army, an evil force like a sweet soothing deadly gas. For years, seeping in through cracks and windows in the slowly built mansion of civilization, it had been rotting our whole moral structure, and now, he said, in the land there is hardly a recognition of any moral authority. In America, particularly at the beginning of the republic, men were fascinated by the idea of freedom. But where do we find freedom? It always begins in choice. A new army, marching by night, a great host, crying love, not war, is fascinated by the peace that can come with surrender. Young men now wallow in the cowardice of this peace. The moral cowardice. Peace with evil. Peace with the death of the spirit, the death here at home, not in the jungles of Vietnam. . . .

"My God," Mark said, leaning back, and then, with a grim hard smile, rapped his knuckles on the paper spread out on the bar. "Well, there he is. There's what you've got now! Solzhenitsyn in short pants," and he stared at the mahogany wall panelling behind Heffernan's head as if the shiny surface had put him in a trance.

Just a few months ago, when he thought of Monk as another father, the reading of such a speech would have broken his heart, but now it gave him a cynical satisfaction. "Isn't it fascinating?" he said. "I could see this coming out in him. I almost had him figured out. Closer and closer to God, he said. And this new freedom. Now it's him and God — if God will only let him get a little closer. Okay, he will! Yes he will, and he'll have a hundred thousand young men killed in the jungle to serve his moral purpose. A wild old man on a white horse riding at the head of his great new constituency. Millions of them, the rednecks, the hard hats, those crummy trendy neo-conservative intellectuals . . ." Then, realizing he was showing his grim satisfaction, he checked himself and said apologetically to Cretia, "You see, Cretia, he's now against everything dear to me."

"Then kill him off. Kill him off," Heffernan said lightly. But Mark, his eyes on Cretia, was shaken. She had started to laugh. Her eyes were shining. He was shocked by the power of Monk's grip on her imagination; it frightened him.

Shrugging, she said almost sympathetically, "It's a position, Mark. It's just a position about a war in Southeast Asia. In Italy, they are more interested in Palestine and the Middle East. Jeremy is simply a conservative. So is the Pope. Are they all a little wild? You are a man of the left, Mark."

"Jeremy. The man of the right? Wow!"

"Oh, left right, left right," she said airily. "Eyes front, left, left, left. Pick it up. Left. He was a good man and he left."

"Have another drink, Cretia."

"I don't need a drink."

"Then tell me what Jeremy's heading for."

"He simply sees what he has to see, the things other people don't see. Anyway, I don't want to talk about this. It's never the real thing."

"What the hell is the real thing?"

"As if you don't know," and she laughed.

"Excuse me," Heffernan said, glancing at Cretia, and then at Mark. "I'm just the observer. The old Flaubertian observer, you know. But it's past midnight and I've got to get some sleep." They agreed to have lunch the next day. Heffernan left, and Cretia said, "And we'll go, too. Come on."

When they left the café, no one was sitting in the cooped-in terrace. It had turned quite cool. On the way to the parked car, walking in step, sometimes brushing against each other, they said nothing, but in the car, going along boulevard du Montparnasse, and just before they got to that blaze of café light at the Raspail corner, he said, "Why did Jeremy drop me, Cretia?"

"He knows things, Mark."

"He knows I love you, Cretia."

"He knows I'm his wife."

"You're not his wife, not his woman. What are you, Cretia?"

Staring straight ahead, she drove into the grey street shadows of Raspail, and leaning against her, he said softly, "I think I loved you the first time I saw you. Not just to get into bed with you. It was your presence, something pervading, something slowly invading, getting into my head without me knowing, then always there and hurting till I pictured you close beside me."

"Jeremy needs me, Mark."

"Jeremy needs God, not you. He's put you aside as a wife."

"He can't put me aside, Mark," she said calmly. "Ah, no, he can't. I've often caught him looking at me in such a strange way, looking at me as I stood beside him, as if he knows I see him now as I saw him in the beginning, and so I'm always there for him to come home to."

They had turned along Vaugirard, stopping at his hotel. They waited a little, her hands still on the wheel. As he went to put his arm around her, she said, "You see, Mark, I've heard from Jeremy, a long talk on the phone. I think he'll be here in Paris for only a few days. Then he wants me to go to the Middle East — to Jordan, and go into the desert — as we did before. He's so excited, a book on his desert reflections. His publisher loves the idea." Pausing, troubled, she sighed. "Oh, I don't know, Mark."

"How long will he be around here?"

"Just four days."

"Four days." As he opened the door, he tried to see the expression on her face and couldn't. "Cretia, listen to me," he said quietly.

"I'll have to go with him," she said.

"I don't like the feel of it, Cretia. It feels all wrong."

"What are you trying to do?"

"Tell you not to go. I've just four days to talk to you."

"You can't talk to me. I won't be seeing you. And don't phone me. Don't make trouble."

"Ah, but I'll be talking to you."

"Oh, Mark, don't be foolish."

"I'll be talking to you."

"Where on earth? How on earth?"

"I'll be talking to you in your dreams," he said quietly. "Wherever I am, I'll suddenly find myself talking to you. I'll reach you."

"Oh sure," she said laughing. "And I'll be listening, waiting, then listening," and again she laughed. "Good night, Mark."

He watched the taillights of her car, and then, entering the hotel, lost in thought, he neither saw nor spoke to the elderly man at the desk. In his room, he undressed quickly, got into bed, turned out the light, but after a few minutes he got up, and without turning on the light, sat in the corner chair and pondered. The room's window faced a side street and the pale street light just reached his bare feet. For a long time, I've sat holding Jeremy Monk's coat, he thought bitterly, and I couldn't believe he had discarded it and was wearing a fine new coat. Then, as he remembered how untouched, how untroubled Cretia had been by his bitter attack on Monk, and how she had even laughed, he grew troubled and tried to understand the nature of her faith in Monk. It was more than a faith. It was as if Monk had made her a part of his whole wild religious fantasy about freedom and God. But Cretia, he thought, Cretia going in for those celibate ecstasies, denying her own nature. Is that Cretia? He sat in the darkness for a long time, then, just as his eyes got used to the light in the room and he could make out the pillow on the bed and the dresser, he stood up, suddenly alert; he thought he had an insight; in the beginning, Monk with his powerful, colourful, ingratiating personality had got into Cretia's imagination. For Cretia, the truth about everything — from gardens to people to painting — was to be found in her imagination. That was Cretia. Monk had captured her imagination. And it could be, he thought, quickening, as he began to pace up and down, that her frightening loyalty was not to Monk, but to her own imagination. This was not as complicated as it might seem. It meant that as soon as Monk did something that violated her imagination — as he surely would the way he was going — he would lose her. The thing to remember, he thought grimly, is that he knows he's got to get her far away from me, and when she sees this, he's a goner.

HEFFERNAN CAME TO THE hotel in the late morning and told Mark that he had seen Monk, who was willing to cooperate and work rapidly on the biography. Heffernan was so full of information about the Monks that Mark suggested meeting for a late lunch at La Coupole. Heffernan was seeing the Monks again before lunch. Monk looked a little thinner, Heffernan said, and seemed very keyed up with a strange inner sense of expectancy that caused him to drift off, smiling sweetly or peacefully to himself. A most remarkable self-directed or God-beckoning man, Heffernan said. Evidently, Monk had been deluged with letters and phonecalls after his Harvard lecture, and the American publisher was counting heavily on his new desert book.

As they parted, Mark said, "Be sure to say hello to Cretia for me," and when Heffernan was gone, he waited. He concentrated on a picture of Cretia with her hand out, taking Heffernan's who said "Mark says hello." And then, closing his eyes, he reached out to her in his thoughts and whispered, Cretia, darling, I love you. You're not going to the Middle East. I know you don't want to go. Stay here, you and I in one another's arms. I love the feel of you, the thought of you. That desert hawk! He's not the man who excited your imagination, he's another man. What have his strange celibate fantasies to do with you? He's trying to change your nature. That's a crime. Nothing real there, nothing real, and the fresh wonder of real things was in you. Don't go, Cretia. I won't let you go.

He bought Heffernan lunch, and he bought him drinks, wanting word about the Monks' plans. He couldn't figure out whether Heffernan believed in Monk. All he would say was, "God-intoxicated men always interest me, Mark. They make good stories." On the third day he said, "Well, here's something that will surprise you. After the desert trip they'll be moving to Rome."

"Rome?" Mark asked, startled. "Why Rome?"

"It's Cretia's hometown, isn't it? She still has that studio on the Via Margutta. Do you know Rome?"

"I don't know Rome. No."

"Via Margutta is not too far away from the Spanish Steps. It's a painters' street. The studios."

"Rome," Mark said softly. "Ah, yes. Yes, indeed."

"No, it's more than that, Mark. Jeremy says he feels it'll be like going home. Sooner or later a man must head for home. The peace of home. Jeremy at last finding his home in Rome. Isn't it funny?"

"He's leaving here Sunday?"

"Sunday afternoon and they're gone."

"Cretia?"

"Of course she's going."

"Is that what she says?"

"Look here, Mark. Why wouldn't she go?"

"Off to the desert again? Why should she go?"

"Really? What do you know that I don't know? Do you want to bet on it?"

"There's no point. I know. I simply know, that's all," and musing to himself, he smiled and nodded and nodded again, and Heffernan, baffled, said, "Are you talking to me or to yourself?"

Heffernan's interest in Cretia was so casual and detached that Mark had concluded he was a homosexual. Then, the night before the Monks were to leave, he was sitting on the terrace of the Deux Magots looking across the square at the church in the darkening shadow. It was a chilly night. He saw Heffernan getting out of a prostitute's car, the prostitute, a pretty blonde with a squirrel stole on her shoulders. There was the usual hooker's car kiss, the hooker leaning out the window, and then, having delivered him to the café, she drove off. So I was all wrong about Heffernan, Mark thought. What else am I wrong about around here? Sitting down, Heffernan said, "She was very nice, Mark," and he began to talk about his real respect for many prostitutes and about his own life with his mother, and how she had raised him, helping him to win a scholarship. He didn't know who his father was and didn't think she did either. Everything he knew about lovemaking, he learned spying on his mother and her lovers. "I used to worry about something bad happening to her. Ah, women, women and their wondrous ways," he said, sighing. "I adored her, so of course I worried about losing her. Haven't you noticed there's always a woman somewhere you worry about losing?"

"That's true, very true," Mark said, thinking about his premonition of a death in the desert. Off by himself, there was an expression of intense concentration on his face as he pictured Cretia and brought her close and said to her in his thought, It's settled, Cretia. I won't let you go.

"Hey, where are you?" Heffernan tugged at his sleeve. "Are we going to dinner later?" He was waiting for Mark to pay for the drinks. He believed Mark had an expense account because Mark had been slipping him a few dollars for bringing him stories about Paris.

It was not a night when Mark wanted to be alone. He took Heffernan to dinner, and afterwards he bought the *New York Times* and they went back to Mark's hotel room. Heffernan, sitting on the floor, spread out *The Times* and read while Mark, stretched out on the bed, thought, Why do

I seem to know that if Cretia goes tomorrow to the Middle East I'll never see her again? Then Heffernan said, "Here's a story for you. And I know more than *The Times*. Look." And Mark, kneeling beside him, read about an eighty-year-old movie actress, Louise Harmon, whose early silent pictures had been rediscovered and how she had become a cult figure because of her mysterious beauty. Now she was called "The Face." Men of three generations had been haunted by the expression on her face. There was a photograph of the young Louise Harmon, a pretty, dark-haired girl with bangs. But it was her eyes that gave her face a haunting mystery, a look that was erotically compelling and yet of another time. "Something in that face," Mark said. "Yeah, it reminds me of Cretia."

"Let's see," Heffernan said, peering at the picture. "No, I don't see Cretia. Not at all. Well, maybe the cheekbones." Louise Harmon now lived in Paris in the Faubourg-St-Honoré. She wouldn't give interviews; she wouldn't be photographed; she hid her face. It was said she was an alcoholic and drank straight from the bottle. "But what I know, and they don't know, is this," Heffernan said brightly. He told Mark he had heard that Louise Harmon came every night from her apartment in the Faubourg-St-Honoré and sat by herself in this one little café in Montmartre. She sat there dreaming and getting happily drunk. At midnight a car would come and drive her back to St-Honoré.

"Great. Let's go to Montmartre," Mark said.

At night, the neighbourhood around Sacré Coeur had a cosy warmth, a village closeness. "The life that was lived here, you feel it. It's like a sacred grove from the last century," Mark said. "You can almost hear things. See faces you should know." They found the little old café.

When Mark entered the café he saw a veiled woman sitting all alone at a corner table, and approaching the plump black-haired woman who sat at the cash register, he asked politely if the lady at the corner table came every night. He thought the madame might be glad to get some publicity for her café. Coming slowly from behind her counter, her hands on her hips, she scowled and said quietly, "*Cochon. Cochon.*" Then, as if galvanized, she grabbed a broom standing at the counter's corner and chased him out to the little terrace, waving her broom. She cried that nothing was sacred to him because he had no shame and, indeed, he was a pig. When he joined Heffernan, who stood across the street laughing, they moved away, deep into the shadows and waited. Then at midnight, a big car came to the café. The driver stood at the open door. The heavily veiled old woman came out and stood framed in the light.

The driver shut the car, and was gone. "Who did she meet here years ago?" Mark asked. "That's the question. At night around here it all seems like years ago. It's all that counts with her now — memories of her private life, the sacred things she kept hidden, and must keep hidden, or they die." Then, with a pang, he thought of Chartres, Cretia and the window in the cathedral, and if, as he now feared, he might never see her again, would Chartres be just a place where something had happened years ago?

They left Montmartre, parted, and though Mark went right to bed, he couldn't sleep. With the dawn, he slept. Early in the afternoon, the ringing telephone woke him. Heffernan said, "I say, old boy, this is astonishing. Cretia did not go with Jeremy. How did you know?"

◊ E I G H T E E N ◊

S HE LAY BACK IN THE chair, he was so full of wonder that he could actually believe Cretia had heard him talking to her in her dreams, or in her meditative moments had heard him warning her not to go. When his wonder passed, he grew exultant. Jumping up, he threw off his pajamas, took a bath, and lay in the tub, smiling to himself. Shaving, he paused and smiled again. When he had dressed, he called Cretia's apartment. She answered and he said softly, "You didn't go."

"No," she said. In the silence that followed, he could hear her breathing, heavy breathing as if she had hurried to the phone from a distance and was out of breath. Finally, she said, "I thought it over, Mark. Something was worrying me. It was strange."

"I was thinking about it, too," he said, "thinking about it all the time."

"I'm not superstitious," she said. "But somehow I knew I shouldn't go to Jordan. I don't know, a foreboding. Something not right for me. I wasn't needed there, I would be in the way. No, more than that, Mark, I didn't think Jeremy should go. I said, 'What's driving you, Jeremy? What's driving you?' Last night when he sat looking at me for a long time, oh, such a long time, I thought he was ready to say he would not go. But he was only trying to understand how I felt, and I think he was satisfied that I should not go with him."

"Oh, good. Can I see you tonight, Cretia?"

"Oh, no, Mark. For God's sake, no."

"No. But why Cretia? Why?"

"Not when I'm feeling this way. Ah, no, Mark," and her voice broke. "I'd be too easy. And it must not be." Then the conversation took a strange turn. Their voices did not seem to be on the phone. They were like whispers in the dark, urgent whispering — as if he were in the bed beside her, his hands on her, his lips on hers, and she was telling him why she couldn't do it. "I know now you have no loyalty to Jeremy," she whispered. "That's all gone. It had to go in you. Don't you see, Mark? Your loyalty was my protection. It held us back. It was a cloak around me, a cloak around you. But now, your loyalty to him is not there, and since I have these strange mixed-up feelings, you could take me to bed so easily. I'd want you to, Mark, and with Jeremy away. But it would be as if I had just been waiting for him to go, telling him I couldn't go, and I'd feel so cheap. Mark dear, listen. While Jeremy's away I don't want to see you. I must not do this to him while he's on this mission. So don't call me; please don't call me and tempt me. I have a feeling of foreboding that bad things may happen to Jeremy in the desert. I know it surely will happen if I'm here in bed with you." These words came from her so breathlessly he could not interrupt her. "Just let me be for a while till Jeremy's safe," she pleaded. "Let me be till the time comes when I call you. Goodbye, Mark," she said firmly and hung up.

"I'll be goddamned," he said, and shattered, he sat listening to the beating of his heart. The beat quickened; his heart was racing. "Fibrillations," he thought. "This has never happened." Then, worried, he stood up, walking around till he felt like himself. "I've been a fool," he said aloud. He had been taken in by his own convictions, his feeling of certainty, a power he had felt. Abashed, confused, he tried to laugh at himself. The joke's on me, he thought. Jeremy Monk did not have to get Cretia far away from him. Monk could remain far away, as he was now, and still call the shots for her. Even though Cretia meant every word she said, this is what it amounted to. So what is it Monk knows about me — knows about her? he wondered uneasily. Then, as he kept pacing up and down, baffled and despairing, he heard a little voice, an ancestral voice, whispering. But that ache in her voice, that ache in her heart, is really there, and she'll have to call. Just wait.

A little later, he got in touch with Heffernan who lived close to the Jethroes, to the old Montparnasse cemetery and asked how long it would be before he heard from Monk. In about two weeks, Heffernan said, but of course, if there were great new spiritual adventures that took Monk with certainty closer to God, he'd come hurrying back to get his book written. "Ah, yes, indeed," Mark said sourly, "and he'll tell how this time he found himself sitting at the right hand of God." "That's good, very good," Heffernan said, "I'll try and use it somewhere." Monk was his friend, a great man, a moral force, and jokes on him, he implied, were to be expected.

While he waited, Mark sought absorption in his own work. He wrote an amusing story on Louise Harmon and the Montmartre Café, telling just how it had happened. He caught up on his reading of European politics, and proposed a story on the strange political influence of jazz in Prague. He also talked to the London bureau about the Pope's recent illness, but Nancy said the word was the Pope would live for a long time. When he returned to his hotel late at night, he asked if there had been any messages for him, and he thought, "She certainly knows her own mind," and then uneasily, ". . .or is it her own mind?" and a week passed.

In the second week, Heffernan said he had a story for him; would he be interested in meeting the great playwright, Sam Beckett? No one got an interview with the reclusive

Beckett, he said, but if Mark's paper was interested, the interview could be arranged almost accidently. "Is it a story?" he asked. "You see, Beckett is my friend."

"Beckett and Monk," Mark said. "At one time I would have linked them. I'd love to talk to Beckett. You're a man who knows everybody, you're wonderful, Heff."

Beckett, the kind of private self-directed man Jeremy Monk had once been, did not give interviews, nor did he ever appear on television. Heffernan said he had not only met Beckett, but occasionally he'd had a drink with him; Beckett drank at the Falstaff, he said. As if by accident, they could stumble upon him there, drinking by himself, and he could introduce Mark. He telephoned Beckett. He came back smiling. "He'll drop into the Falstaff tomorrow afternoon. How about that?"

At the right hour, they went to the Falstaff. Beckett wasn't there. Next day, they tried again. The bartender said Beckett had been in an hour earlier. It was the same the following day. Trying three times more, Heffernan urged the bartender to phone as soon as he saw Beckett come into the bar. With dignity, the bartender said he couldn't violate Sam's privacy. Mark said, "Heffernan, maybe he phones Beckett when he sees you coming."

"There is no explanation, absolutely no explanation. Beckett is my friend," Heffernan said sternly. Mark grew sour. "The explanation is that there is no explanation," he said. "Very Beckettian. I don't think Beckett is laughing at you. This is called Waiting for Beckett. You stay here, my poor baffled buddy. You may be Beckett's friend, but maybe not his best friend. Beckett, the godless man, has no public face. He preserves his mysterious vision and his abyss. On the other hand, Monk is your spiritual man. He'll see you every day, won't he? — everybody but me," and he went back to his hotel where the desk clerk handed him a message. He was to call Cretia.

The phone rang only once, and she answered, and at the sound of his voice complained plaintively, "Where were you? I called three times." Astonished, he said he had been working on a story. "Why are you so upset? Every day I thought you might call." Sounding more like herself she said, "It's all right now, Mark. I'm supposed to be out at Orly Airport in two hours. I'm leaving for Rome. I thought I'd have to go without seeing you. It upset me. I wanted you to call for me and drive with me to the airport."

He didn't go up to his room. He hurried out to the street and stood at the curb, waving at passing taxis that didn't stop; then one that passed and was well down the street, turned and came back. The sky was darkening. In two minutes, when he saw the St Sulpice towers against this darkening sky, he felt a touch of sadness, an intimation that this neighbourhood, the four cafés not far from the cathedral, their lights coming on, was about to be lost to him forever. At the Monk apartment, he told the driver to wait. Cretia, standing at the open door, was wearing a brown leather skirt and a black turtleneck sweater. "Mark, bless you," she said, both her hands out, and he took both hands and kissed them, saying nothing. It was a courtly dignified moment. She had three heavy bags which he carried to the taxi. "Well, we'll make it all right," he said, and as he sat beside her in the taxi, her grip on his arm tightened.

"You want to know why I'm so upset. Well, I got a call from Amman just before noon from Jeremy. He didn't sound like himself at all, Mark. I'm sure he got into some kind of trouble, something so shattering he couldn't sound like himself. He said he had been ill for a couple of days in Amman. Ill in the hotel, but was all right now, except that he had to get home. And he had to know that I'd be there in Rome waiting for him to come home. I don't know. Maybe I couldn't hear everything he said. I thought he sounded a little shaken. Do you know, Mark, I've never heard his voice break like that. And then, so much more like himself, he said he had known all along there was a warm place waiting for him in Rome."

"Worried about you," he said softly. "Far away, but now worried about you."

"Not just about me, Mark."

"About losing you. Yes, losing you."

"He was ill, lying in a hotel room ill."

"And at last — not sure of himself."

"Don't be a brute, Mark. This is not you."

"You're here and I'm here. He gets you away quick. That's not like him, Cretia. Ah, no. Well, good."

Riding in the gathering darkness, she sat stiffly beside him, but clutched his hand, and though she held on, he knew all her concern was for Monk, and suddenly as he saw this, he quickened; he thought he saw a change in her, something new in the way she saw Monk. Now Monk wasn't in charge of her. Whatever she had heard from Amman, it made her want to console and protect Monk. A weakened Monk, needing her with him! As they rode along in silence, he was trying to figure out what to do. Just before they got to the airport, she handed him a card, her Via Margutta address. "Be sure to write to me, Mark," she said. At the airport, helped by the driver, he got her bags on a carriage and rolled them to the ticket counter. The airport was crowded. Pushing the luggage, he nearly bumped into an old woman in a wheelchair. The apologies took time. At the desk, she turned, her arms came around him and she kissed him, a slim girl in a leather skirt and black sweater with an easy athletic assured stride, hurrying away, but before entering the escalator tunnel, she turned, her hand up, and as she vanished, he felt a wrench, not just at his heart, but at his whole being, such a wrench that he was left weak and trembling, wanting to cry out after her. Then, angry at himself, he thought, What am I? This manocuvring. At home I would never take this, and the thoughts he had been fumbling with, in the taxi, suddenly took shape.

As SOON AS HE GOT BACK to the hotel he called the airline, booked a seat on a supper-flight to Rome leaving Paris the next day and talked to the desk clerk about Roman hotels. In the end, he telephoned the Excelsior on the Via Veneto and made a reservation. After trying to call Nancy Holman at his London bureau without getting her, and trying, too, to reach her at home, he went to bed. In the morning, he talked to Nancy. He was off to Rome, he said, and would be there in a few hours and could be reached at the Excelsior. Laughing, and imagining he wanted to be in Rome to write stories on the death of the Pope, she said, "Aren't you rushing it a little, Mark? We hear that the Pope, who is at Castel Gandolpho, has taken a turn for the better and may soon be up and around." However, since he was going on his own, he wouldn't be on an expense account, she said. She hoped, just the same, that he would like Rome.

He came to Rome at late twilight when the last of the sun's rays had vanished and a bluish mist hung over the ancient city. Checking into the hotel, he had no complicated plans. All he wanted to do was drop in on Monk and Cretia. Standing at the hotel entrance, he looked across the Via Veneto to the Café de Paris where all the tables on the terrace were under pink awnings, and then to the left, at Doney's, where the movie people from Cinecitta used to sit. But time had passed. The people who now sat at Doney's were aging citizens who watched the passing sidewalk crowd, hoping to recognize some troubled celebrity, as if they were the jury there to judge of his life.

At that hour, the Via Veneto was a busy wide street. The trees were full of thousands of chirping birds. Well-dressed men with tanned, travelled faces came sauntering by, and pretty young women in sweater-coats, ready for the chill in the air around midnight. On the corner across from Harry's Bar, two hookers, never soliciting, stood there as if they were a civic service. Crossing the street, he sat down on the terrace of the Café de Paris. The barrel-chested waiter with a mop of curly black hair and a boyish face, spoke to him in English. "How did you know to speak to me in English?" Mark asked. "I can always tell," the waiter said proudly. "I lived in Brooklyn. For two years I lived in Brooklyn." After he had brought Mark a drink, a Campari and soda, a drink he had never ordered any other place, the waiter explained he had returned to Rome because he had missed his wife and mother. Now he would like to go back to Brooklyn. He helped Mark to feel at home and sure of himself. But he didn't know how far he was from Cretia's place. Remembering that Heffernan had said, "Not far from the Spanish Steps, and the Via Condotti . . . ," he asked the waiter where the Spanish Steps were. Pointing along the street, the waiter said he could walk along a block, then turn left down a street of little boutiques and keep on to the end of the street, then turn left and keep on going, and soon — in about half an hour — he would be at the top of the Spanish Steps, looking down at the fountain and the nearby Via Condotti. "That's wonderful," Mark said. "Just the same, I think I'll take a taxi."

"There," the waiter said. "Move quick."

A taxi had stopped at the café, and Mark, after waiting at the curb for a slim woman and a middle-aged man wearing pearl-grey gloves to get out, gave the driver the Via Margutta address. It was dark, a full darkness, but the Via

Veneto was a blaze of light, and there were racing motor-
cycles and yelling and some wild laughter. Untouched by the
lights or the sound, Mark sat stiffly, a grim little smile on his
face, anticipating the encounter ahead with Monk. When the
taxi stopped at the address, he had a little difficulty paying
the driver; he wasn't accustomed to lire, and then he stood
on the pavement looking at a three-storeyed well-kept old
building. In the vestibule were mailboxes and names. Signora Jeremy Monk was on the second floor. Climbing the
stairs, he wavered for the first time, and stopping, took a
deep breath, then, mounting the stairs, the sound of his own
step gave him satisfaction. There was a knocker on the door.
He knocked. He heard someone singing, Cretia singing. He
knocked three times more, impatiently. Then the door
opened. She was there, staring at him. Wearing a simple blue
dress low on her shoulders, she had on high heels and had a
comb in her hand. "Mark, what in hell is this?" she said.

"Can't I come in?"

"Come in. Yes. Come in. Where did you come from?
What is this Mark?" she asked uneasily. "Why are you here?"

"You're here," he said calmly. "I'm here. You're in Rome,
I'm in Rome. What's the matter with that? Where's Jeremy?"

"He gets in tonight."

"Gets in from where? Amman?"

"And Petra. He was in Petra."

"Is there really such a place, a rose-red Petra?"

"There is."

"I thought he'd be here," he said, confused for a moment
about his own intentions.

"Why don't you just go, Mark? You know how awkward
it'll be if you're here."

"I had no intention of staying, Cretia," he said. "I just
dropped in to say hello. Neighbourly gesture. I'm here in
Rome. Just thought he'd like to know I'm here in Rome. I
just dropped in. Take it easy," but he was walking slowly

around the big studio. A window as big as Jethroe's looked over the street, the upper half shining with moonlight. On the wall to the right, a small Matisse and a larger Chagall, and in the corner, a stack of unframed canvases. A rust-coloured couch sat against the wall under the Matisse. "In Paris Jeremy never asked me to come around, did he? He dropped me," he said calmly, still moving around and not looking at her. "He doesn't like me being around. Well, even in Rome I'm here. What if he goes with you to Baluchistan and finds me there, just there?" and he laughed.

Listening, she watched him, feeling herself pulled to him, and she went to speak, but couldn't. Her eyes moist and shining, she said softly, "To come here just because I'm here. To be here even though you might never be able to see me. Oh, Mark." Her eyes turned inward, then, trying to laugh, she put out her hands. As he took her hands, they both froze, startled by the heavy tolling of a great bell. The slow heavy solemn clanging came rolling up from the square at St Peter's, bringing mournful echoes to all the hills of Rome. Shaken, he said, "What is it? What's happening? Cretia!"

"It means the Pope is dead," she said, and came closer to him. Just listening, he held her. They were both unnerved, as if the tolling came not just out of this one Roman night but out of all the layers of life that had been lived around those hills for thousands of years, and they were filled with loneliness and wonder that they were together on such a night. She shivered. Suddenly she took his head in both her hands and kissed him, then kissed him again. He took her in his arms and carried her over to the wide couch. With the bell still tolling, he covered her with kisses, his hands groping for her, and he had her; then suddenly, she grabbed his hands. It was as if the vast silence that followed the tolling of the bell had shocked her. Her grip on his hands was strong! As her eyes met his, her face was burning, she was trembling, but she said, "I won't. I won't. I can't." Bewildered, then angry, ready to grab her savagely, he said, "No, goddamn it, no." She released his hands, then gravely slipped the shoulder strap of her dress from the left shoulder, and drew out her breast. While his mouth was on her nipple, she watched him intently, making little movements with her own lips, her eyes full of nurturing gentleness.

Finally she said, "It's time you left here, Mark," and calmly drew her breast away from him, slipping it back under her dress. "You mustn't be here when Jeremy comes in. Oh, not now. Oh, Lord, not now." But he lay there trying to figure out how she could really believe she had kept her loyalty to Monk by keeping him out of her one last secret place.

"You're right," he said finally. "Now I don't want to be here when he comes in." He ran his hands through his hair. She smoothed out her dress and picked up the comb she had had in her hand when he came to the door. It had fallen on the floor.

"Tell me where you are staying," she asked.

"At the Excelsior. Will you call me?"

"I'll call you, if I can."

"Promise me."

"I'll try and call you, but I'll have to see."

"Do one thing for me, Cretia."

"What's that?"

"Be sure and tell Jeremy I wanted to see him, but I couldn't stay. I just dropped in."

"Oh, I'll tell him," she said, and they were at the door. "Good night, Mark."

"Good night," he said. "Look, Cretia, it doesn't really matter that I didn't see him," he said. "He'll know I'm here in Rome," and he laughed. "It'll spook him."

"Spook him?"

"That's right."

"Oh, Mark. Really," she said. But she had an alarmed expression in her eyes.

◊ T W E N T Y ◊

———————————

BY THE AFTERNOON OF the next day, Nancy Holman was in the Ambasciatori hotel. She was very busy. She brought word from Harold Hines: he was to write a general colour story on the Pope and the Roman crowds. He would be on an expense account. She had brought funds from London. She, herself, would look after the hard news. She became briskly competent. Even her kiss, though generous, was brisk and to the point. She assumed that he accepted her as his boss, though she had no control over his time or his work. Leaving her talking on the phone to the interpreter, hired through the hotel, a patrician woman writer with time on her hands who lived in Parioli, Mark went out to get his bearing. There was a very blue sky and strong sunlight and an enchanting blue haze still hung over the city, and he took a taxi to St. Peter's to see the great square and look at the obelisk and at Bernini's great colonnade around the square, and as he came out of the square the twilight faded quickly into darkness. He could hardly see the Tiber or Hadrian's Tomb, and then it got very dark and he couldn't find a taxi and felt like a stranger in an ancient city that had its own darkness, its own smell, which was not like the smell of Paris; this was a murkier, earthier smell of lived-in old houses and dust.

He told himself he would find a message from Cretia when he got back to the hotel. There was no message. No one had asked for him. A little later, he sat in Nancy's room with the interpreter, a fine-featured silver-haired woman of forty-five who lived on the Via Archimede, the street where Cretia's father lived. She did not know Cretia, she said, but knew her father, a wise, knowing man who was able to defend himself. He asked the signora what did the death of a Pope mean to the wise girls of the Via Veneto. "Come with me," Signora Ferraro said, and led him to the Café de Paris, and upstairs to the bar where she whispered to a platinum-haired girl with elegant long legs wearing an expensive black suit and a white fur piece — by profession, a companion she said — and then introduced him.

Of course, they were deeply involved with the Pope's death, the elegant woman insisted. The Pope was not just Christ's vicar on earth; for Romans, he was their "Papa," and though he might be good or bad as a politician or a teacher, nevertheless, he was their "Papa," just as in a family, you sometimes got mad at the Pope, but you don't like it when Papa dies. Then Nancy Holman, her day's work done, came into the bar and said she was hungry. They took a taxi to Alberto's in Trastevere for a late supper. At supper Nancy agreed the signora could work for him, showing him around, for two hours after lunch. When he returned to the hotel, he asked again at the desk if there had been any messages. That night, he dreamt he saw Cretia being turned away at the door of the hotel. Next day, when he was with the signora standing by Bernini's fountain at the foot of the Spanish Steps, and she was explaining why she took on work as a translator — "One can always use a little extra money" — he said, "Wait," startling her. "Look at that girl coming along the Via Condotti. Look at the way she walks, the carriage, the set of her shoulders, the head erect, the face. How does this happen?" Shrugging, the signora said that maybe such women carried jars or baskets on their heads two thousand years ago. "The face? I don't know." A little later, he stood transfixed again; he believed he had caught a glimpse of Cretia's face in another pretty young woman coming up the Via Condotti. A Modigliani neck, and there — getting out of a car, a Botticelli face. He began to believe, too, that he would see Cretia, herself, since she lived nearby, coming out of one of the expensive stores into the autumn sunlight. But the signora went back to Nancy, and he went to the Press Club on the Via della Mercede.

In the Press Club, there was a narrow room extending from the entrance, and a long bar crowded with journalists from many cities. Beyond the bar was a wide room with tables and chairs. Upstairs, typewriters clicking all day long. Standing near the end of the bar, with two men between him and a view of the big lounge, he got into conversation with a middle-aged newspaperman from one of the American weeklies. The two men at the end of the bar left. The middle-aged newspaperman said suddenly, "Did you know Jeremy Monk was in there?"

"Jeremy Monk. In where?"

"At the back. Behind that big table with those three guys. Can you see him?"

"I can see him," Mark said.

Jeremy Monk sat erect and unsmiling, and though he was being talked to, he obviously wasn't listening. The newspapermen didn't seem to mind his indifference. They were flattered that he was there, one of them on their big international story. He had on a stylish blue denim jacket and a blue shirt. A newspaperman moved; Mark got a good look at Monk. "What's he doing here?" he asked.

"He'll get a big story out of this; he's got a lotta talent, that guy," the man from the American weekly said. "He'll get read."

"You bet he will," Mark said sourly. "And it'll be his own story, not the dear dead Pope's. What's he doing here?"

"What does he do? Nothing. Just sits and looks around."

"Seeing who's here?"

"Maybe he's supposed to meet someone." Mark half turned; Monk was still there, aloof, bored, impassive, occasionally peering over a shoulder to watch someone come in, and he looked lonely. Aloof and very lonely, and Mark thought, "Cretia has told him I'm here. Is he really looking for me?"

The middle-aged journalist left and Mark, though fifty feet away, was in Monk's direct line of vision. Seeing him, Monk stood up quickly, and brushing by a man trying to talk to him, he came toward the bar. Averting his eyes, Mark turned away, giving no sign of recognition. He knew it was time to get away. "Yeah, spooked!" Mark thought. "Excuse me. Got to go," he said to the bartender and hurried out, along the Via della Mercede, not looking back, certain Monk had followed him to the street, hoping to catch him at the curb, looking for a taxi. At the street corner, he went back a few steps, though still out of sight, and saw Monk, a lonely figure at the curb. My God, what does he want from me? Then he grew angry at himself for being so shaken. "What is this?" he thought and strode away.

The man he was walking away from had been his spiritual father. For years, he thought, and look at him, lonely, and troubled, a lonely ascetic. But my own father was not a lonely man, not like that at all. Pigheaded, opinionated, ruthless, cynical, a snob, he might have been, and he was intolerant, too. But he was charming and perceptive — if he had to be. He was hard to love, but not hard to hate. Yet beyond a doubt, those had been his qualities when he'd written his Paris diary. As a young painter, a man of appetites and pigheaded convictions, looking for something new, he hadn't tried to change his temperament. No, he had changed the direction of his life, and maybe because he felt he had to. Maybe he had finally decided he had no real talent, and faced the discovery, hating the failure of his dream of himself, and in a natural bitter disappointment, in his discovery of a lack of authentic talent, he had turned his back forever on the things he knew he couldn't have. Rimbaud also ended up a businessman. But my father was still true to his own outrageous temperament, as mother knew, knowing him better than I did, loving him till the day she died. And he loved her till his death. Hurrying along, he felt closer to his own father than he had ever been, and going into the hotel, he looked around warily, half expecting to see Monk there, waiting. He asked at the desk if there had been any messages. No calls. No messages.

Early next afternoon, when he was with Nancy at the Pope's funeral procession, he was sure he would see Monk among the newspapermen. But it was impossible to look for anyone. Cars were jammed along all roads leading to the square; the streets were crowded with people making their way to the wide avenue of the Conciliazione leading to the square. Mark and Nancy had press passes which entitled them to be inside the barricades where they could look down the great avenue. The sky was still very blue and in the strong afternoon sunlight, the yellow ochre walls of all the old buildings, so drab in wet weather, had turned golden: Rome in the sunlight, now a golden city of ancient temples, splashing fountains and obelisks set down in valleys between green hills. Then came the solemn measured desolate booming of the death bell, and between the massive strokes, the faraway roll of muffled drums. "Look," Nancy said suddenly. Far down the great avenue, the *cortége* — having left St John Lateran over an hour before — came into sight in the sunlight along the Via delle Conciliazone. With the desolating hammering of the bells came strange patches of coloured lights and shadows on the avenue. Out of these patches of light and shadow, as if from a time long past, the antique procession moved along. Then Mark saw figures moving on the roof of St Peter's. Newspapermen, favoured ones, watching, and Monk would be there with Cretia watching alongside him, Mark thought, as the *carabiniere* came on, marching to the slow muffled drumbeat. Petra! She said there still was a rose-red Petra. Behind the *carabiniere*, the red-uniformed noble guard in bearskins and white doeskin breeches marched in the sunlight that kept flashing and dancing on the Pope's glass-walled hearse. They came on, a wavering but endless line, the church prelates, the relatives, the clergy, then the barefoot Franciscans blistering their feet on the hard pavement, the white-robed Dominicans, the ordinary priests, all flowing into the wide open waiting arms of Bernini's great colonnade around the square.

Later, much later, when twilight was on the edge of darkness, he came back alone to the square to view the dead Pope lying in state. In the square, a great gathering of mourners, at least a hundred thousand, were all held back behind trellises, and kept a full seventy paces from the great doors. It was a Roman crowd, mainly middle-aged or older, with no flash of colour in dress, no women from the Via Veneto; just a shadowed sea of funeral faces. Every fifteen minutes, the church doors opened, *carabiniere* would swing back the barricades, and at least two thousand, those closest to the barricade, ran headlong toward the open doors that were already closing against them. Using his press pass, Mark was allowed to crawl under a trestle, and he crossed the open space just as darkness fell and the moon rose. The doors had been opened. The mob charged. The sound of the pounding feet behind him made him turn, frightened. The moon shone on the strange excited ruthless faces coming at him. Jumping, he hurled himself against the stone wall, the church. He hugged the wall. As the mob in the dark came thudding up the steps, he froze in utter panic. He had no heartbeat, his mind bursting in a crazy light, and then, before his eyes closed, he caught a glimpse of a narrowing strip of light. They were closing the door. Hugging the wall, he made his way toward the light, and then, just five feet from the door, he brushed against a tall thin girl in a grey suit who remained, flattened, against the wall. Grabbing her arm, he pulled her along and as the big door closed, he thrust his press pass at the guard. They were allowed to squeeze in. Though he still held the girl's arm he hardly looked at her. Standing by Michelangelo's *Pietà* in the golden splendour of the cathedral, he was aghast that he could have been so shaken.

"Utter panic," he said to the young woman.

"Me too," she said.

"Who are you?" he asked.

"Myrna Shields, the *St Louis Post Dispatch.*"

"Mark Didion, the *Toronto Star*," he said and as they got into the line slowly surging up the centre aisle past the dead Pope's bier on the high altar that was marked by Bernini's twisting black columns, he said, "You look very tired."

"I am," she said. "I've had other things on my mind that set me up for that mob out there. I'm having a terrible time." Her grey suit had a simple elegance. There was a grey streak in her hair. She was about forty. A few years ago she might have been very pretty and still could have been, but her drawn face was full of worry; her nervous mouth kept twisting. She had been in Paris, she said, doing a series on fall fashions for her paper when news came that the Pope was near death. Her paper had asked her to go to Rome, and they were to send funds, care of American Express. Though she had been in Rome for three days, no funds had come. She had found a little place to live, but she was broke, worried and lonely. He told her she looked as if she needed a drink. She said she was sure she did, so when they had gone up the centre aisle, sharing a wonder at this great cavern of art, they came down the side aisle and hurried across the wide steps out of the reach of the ruthless crowd, and on to the taxi stand. In fifteen minutes, they were sitting under a pink awning at the Café de Paris.

It was the lively hour on the Via Veneto. Pretty women in sweater-coats or leather jackets joked with each other at the brightly lit entrance. Weary wise men of forty, whether from Spain, Germany or France, all with the same hunter's eyes, sauntered by, watching and waiting. Myrna said she would like a rum and coke if he would have one with her. She gulped down her drink. "Don't let me stop you, Myrna," he said. "Have another."

"What's the matter with you?" she asked, as she took a third rum and coke. And then, sighing, her eyes a little wild, she said, "You know you could take me home if you wanted to, don't you?" In her loneliness and insecurity, she would like to be home and even weeping in someone's arms, though incredibly, she was not drunk, and he smiled and patted her hand.

Then, from the Excelsior Hotel across the street, Jeremy Monk, still in the blue suit-jacket, his white hair shining in the headlight of a passing car, came to the café terrace. After looking around, he sat down by himself ten feet from Mark.

Mark said to Myrna, "Well, are you ready?"

"Yes, I'm ready," she said, and smiling warmly, she stood up. Taking her arm, he led her to a taxi stand, but as Mark reached the taxi, he could feel Monk's eyes on him, watching him flee. Opening the taxi door, helping Myrna in, he felt a pang, a shame, a stab of anger at himself. "Wait a minute, Myrna," he said. Pulling lire from his pocket he thrust the notes into her hand. "That's to pay for the taxi," he said. He took her head in his hands and kissed her warmly. "Come to the Press Club tomorrow. I'm sorry, Myrna, there's someone at a table looking for me. He's seen me. I'm so sorry. I have to see him." Disconsolate, Myrna said, "Oh, no," and seemed ready to cry, but Mark closed the door. As the cab pulled away, he walked back to the table where Monk, who had not taken his eyes off him, waited.

"Hello, Jeremy," he said casually. "I was sure it was you crossing the street."

"You were with a lady," Monk said. "I knew you had seen me," and he smiled, "but I didn't like to intervene."

His smile was accompanied by a nervous twitch under his left eye. His eyes shifted around as if he suspected someone might be watching him. The skin on his high-cheekboned face, always tightly drawn so that he seemed youthful, now — since he had lost weight — aged him. He looked to be all white hair, and high cheekbones, his blue eyes troubled and restless. Yet, he had kept his air of dignity. In spite of himself, Mark wanted to see the old puckish grin.

"How are you feeling?" he asked. "How's your Vietnam War doing, Jeremy?"

Unruffled, Monk said, "Around here, they're taken up with Palestine and the Middle East."

"You'll do something about that, won't you, Jeremy?"

Still unruffled, Monk said, "I haven't been here. I was in the east, you know. At Petra. You don't know Petra? No one goes to Petra. Rose-red Petra. Well, I think I had been driving myself too hard, running everywhere. It seems to have caught up with me. Something hit me. Sudden exhaustion, I think. Yes, that's it, Mark. They said I suffered from exhaustion. I'm all right now, Mark."

"And you're writing the story here?" Mark asked.

"On the death and birth, yes. The dead Pope and the one to be elected."

"And of course the new Pope will see Jeremy Monk."

"You think so?"

"You're a great public figure now, Jeremy. Who else should he use?"

"Public figure, and not like I was, eh Mark?" and he smiled.

"Well, I'm not like I was either."

"And is Cretia like she was?" he asked gently.

"I don't know," Mark said awkwardly. "How is Cretia?"

"She's fine, Mark. I'm sorry I missed you when you dropped in. Isn't it odd that we're both here on the same story? In the beginning, our first meeting was so innocent, wasn't it? That evening at La Coupole, remember?"

"I could never figure it out, Jeremy. I was a nobody. Why did you take me along with you?"

"A young nobody sitting there in your chair on the boulevard, full of wonder. Ah, the expectation of Montparnasse, just as I had done at your age."

"Yeah, so you said."

"But you weren't a nobody, Mark. You were so open, so full of insight, telling me that wherever I went and no matter what I wrote I would always be my mysterious self. What music that was for an aging man! You enchanted me, Mark. The young enchanter."

"Oh, come on, Jeremy. You knew even then you were off on another track."

"But my own track — and I thought — as you thought, it had to be that way, Mark," but he was cut off by the loud honking of motorbikes, and then more honking and yelling. The waiter brought them drinks and left them in an uneasy silence that fell between them. Monk actually cracked his knuckles. Never having seen him do this, Mark grew uneasy, feeling some terrible tension in him.

"I know you had a bad time in Amman," he said.

"Yes, I was laid up there for a couple of days. I was supposed to have caught a desert chill. My nerves upset and so on. It wasn't a desert chill, Mark."

"No? What was it?"

"Petra. The desert road to Petra. The whole thing." Leaning close, his eyes haunted, his voice breaking, he looked very sad and lonely.

It had suddenly turned chilly. Three people sitting at the next table got up and left. Hardly anyone was left on the terrace. Three girls and two men, coming to the café, went inside and up the stairs to the bar. A rapt expression had settled on Monk's face, and then he nodded, and nodded again. "We started out from Amman," he said. "From Amman, the road led to the desert," and then Mark, looking at him, dared not interrupt while he had that rapt expression on his face.

IN AMMAN," HE SAID, "I hired a small old truck, old because all transportation there seems old, but it had a canvas top and sideboards, a protection against storms, and along with the truck I hired a guide, a Bedouin, a man of about thirty-five dressed in a slick contemporary suit, black pointed shoes and an Arab woollen headcloth, a *keffiyeh*. I couldn't get his right name. I called him Hassan. When Cretia was with me and we went into the desert, we went west toward Egypt. Beyond the rubble, there had been sand, dunes of sand. But now, this was harsher desert, the place of truly deeper desolation where there wasn't even real sand, but I wanted to see the fabled rose-coloured Petra. Our truck packed with supplies and blankets, we drove one hundred and eight miles south to that place which is the beginning of the ancient caravan route from Egypt to Petra. Great business had been done on this route four thousand years ago, and they say that even Moses went along that route to prosperous Petra. Now the route is desert, a hard barren broken-rock stretch that makes the Sahara seem a friendly place of soft warm sand. There were some low bleak hills and some brush, but all around a vast sweep of rubble, and instead of sand, a kind of gravel and piles of dust from the gravel. When the wind blows, this grit cuts the face; it becomes intolerable. As we chugged along in the old truck mile after mile, sudden gusts of wind filled the air with gravel dust which in the sunlight became a shifting yellow mist, a yellow greyness wrapped around us, a greyness which gradually enters a man's soul. In mid-afternoon, out of nowhere appeared four horsemen in *keffiyehs* who stopped us and made us get out of the truck. They weren't robbers. They were some kind of Jordanian militia. Hassan argued with them and, asking for my passport, showed it to them. He invited them to inspect every article in the truck, which they did, and then they were gone. I don't know where they went. But you know, I was glad that they had appeared out of nowhere, yelled and halted us, and then, moved off against the sky. They threw a human shadow on that grey dead world.

"Hassan explained that we would have to watch out for robber bands coming from behind those low ridges. Robbers were always watching the ancient route. And it was getting colder, or rather a chill coming out of the gravel and rubble seemed to enfold us. I did not want to lose the sun before we got to Petra. On we went till we had a flat tire. Imagine a Bedouin with black pointed shoes changing the tire on an old car in the rubble."

A bus, filled with shouting, whooping passengers, came along the Via Veneto. "My God, what's that?" Mark asked.

"Soccer fans," the passing waiter said.

"Soccer fans? Where from?"

"I don't know," the waiter said.

Monk hadn't looked up at the bus. It was as if he hadn't heard the cries and laughter.

"We went on," he said, "deeper and deeper into this harsh and hostile desert till we saw ahead great rocks, the hills around Petra, though there was no sign of the ancient city, nothing ahead but great jutting rocks and then, as we got closer, we saw there was a great cleft in the rocks, the cleft shaped like a vagina, and we went into the deep dark shadows of the cleft. Then, suddenly, we came into a vast open sunlit space sheltered there like a great womb, this womb having its own mysterious light. Ahead was a vast flat stretch of gravel and rubble and piles of dust. Around the great flat area were astonishing cliffs, and carved into the faces of the cliffs were doors and windows, row upon row, like a modern apartment building. And temples were carved in the rock, a city life carved in the rocks, rising among dwelling places. And in the last of the sunlight, the ancient rock city took on a rosy red glow. In that light, with the enveloping shimmering dust screen, many coloured ribbons of light kept floating across the rosy cliff.

"Driving into the great sheltered space, we got out of the car and looking around, I choked with emotion, awed by the mystery, the magnitude, the wonder of man on this earth, and all his works that could come to emptiness and dust. Just think, four thousand years ago there had been bells in those carved temples, bells ringing and children playing and caravans coming in from Egypt and a great market-place where we stood. Now, not a skeleton, not a bone, and worse, a feeling of certainty that even the ghosts had gone. A place now too empty, too desolate even for ghosts. I said to Hassan that I'd like to look into some of the doors in the cliff dwellings. Robbers could be hiding there, he said. While we walked closer to the cliffs, the sun suddenly vanished, clouded over, dark clouds were swept overhead. A wind came up. In a little while the wind came whistling through the great cleft, the entrance, the whistling growing shriller. Taking me by the arm, Hassan headed for the truck where he buckled down the canvas and put our blankets on the floor. The hills, the cliffs, that walled us in, sheltered us from the terrible dust storm, but not from the howling wind. An hour passed, two hours, then came the real night darkness and the screeching coming through the cleft was the shrieking of demons. Hassan said he would not drive out till the storm was over.

"We had flashlights. I tried to sleep. Far into the night I woke up. I think it was the new sudden painful silence that woke me. I used my flashlight. I was alone in the truck. Alarmed, I got out and looking around, wondered if I should call out to Hassan. Actually, I was afraid to hear my own voice, the new vast silence and the starlight seemed to be pressing against my skull. I couldn't bear to look at the moonlit cliff and those empty window spaces. I had never felt such loneliness as in this place that was deserted even by the dead. In this primal darkness, I was afraid to try and move or make a sound. Then terror, no not terror, sheer panic hit me. I froze, I was trembling, and I wanted to scream or die. Then Hassan, coming out of the shadows where he had been relieving himself, called out. My relief so weakened me I couldn't answer or move. Hassan pointed to the dawn light in the sky. Back in the truck we stayed awake. Hassan ate; I couldn't move. Hassan tells me that going back to Amman I held on desperately to the armrest, staring straight ahead."

After a silence that was painful to Mark, Monk said, "I had said I felt I was getting closer to God. I was, Mark. Oh, I knew I was. That's why I said so publicly. The closer I got, the feeling of peace, of confidence, an inner serenity, a divine expectation, getting a little closer all the time. And then, there in Petra, the sudden vast desolate dark loneliness in Petra, the panic. The terrible humiliating panic in the heart, in the head, and the shriek that couldn't come out, and then the flash . . . I had got too close to God. Now God could see me. God looked at me, Mark; I knew he didn't like what he saw."

Drawing himself up, there was a sudden dignified lifting of the still striking white head, and the gesture made Mark want to weep.

"Vanity, vanity, Mark," he said. "The real thing is, a man must know what's right for him. A man must not sin against himself."

"Well, give me time," Mark said quickly. "I may do it too."

"It's the real betrayal, Mark."

"There's a Judas in us all, isn't there?"

"Is there, Mark? Believing! The terrible tyranny in believing. What it can do to a man. Yet a man must believe in himself," he said, his voice shaking, "but not so that he goes against his own temperament."

"I see," Mark said.

Then, for the first time, Monk managed his puckish grin. "Why tell you this? Because you've been important to me, Mark."

"God knows you've been important to me, Jeremy."

"So let's have dinner tomorrow night," he said. "You and me and Cretia."

"The three of us?"

"Cretia will be delighted, I know," he said. "We can meet here, right here at eight tomorrow night. Is it a date?"

"It'll be nice seeing you together," Mark said, and Monk stood up, shook hands warmly and hurried away.

Crossing the street to the hotel, Mark went to his room, got into bed and tried hard to get to sleep, but he was in turmoil. Long after midnight, the crazy honking sounds from the Via Veneto went on, the screeching of motorbikes, the yelling, and a woman's loud wild half-shriek of a laugh faded into the blare of horns, and in the blare he heard Monk's voice: "A man must know what is right for him." His own temperament, Mark thought, cultivate his own garden. But the soil in each man's garden was different. Seeds falling on some soil wouldn't grow. Flowers bloomed in some gardens, wilted and died in others. One's own temperament, and the soil in one's own garden. Mary, Mary quite contrary, how does your garden grow . . . and then he was asleep.

◊ TWENTY-TWO ◊

IN THE MORNING IT RAINED, and in the rain the city was dun-coloured, a flower waiting to open to a golden sun. Mark spent the afternoon in the Press Club helping Nancy Holman put together some short news stories. He looked for Myrna Shields. She wasn't there. In the afternoon, the weather cleared, the sun shone. Then there was another mild fall night. At eight, when Mark was at the café talking to his waiter, he saw Cretia get out of a taxi. He waved and she came hurrying to him. She wore a fine leather jacket and underneath the jacket, a rose-coloured silk dress. The colour for a moment upset him. She whispered, "Mark, oh Mark." He said, "Cretia," and that was all, as if in silence they could say what they wanted to say. Touching her lips with his fingers, he asked, "Where's Jeremy?"

"He'll be along," she said.

"You know about Petra?"

"He told me all about Petra. I'm exhausted, Mark. I'll fall asleep on you. I was up half the night, I'm beat. It was a terrible experience for him, and now it is for me."

"Jeremy's working now, isn't he?"

"Oh, he is. The Pope should be a great story. How did he look to you?" she asked, and then went on: "He took a long walk. He walked by himself this morning in the Borghese Gardens. He told me he sat under an old tree and watched the children playing. A great place to do his thinking, he says."

"What did he say about me, Cretia?"

"He doesn't need to say anything. When he heard you had dropped in he was silent for a long time. Then he said mildly, 'I wish I had been here.'"

"Tonight, Cretia, he'll see that I think of you all the time."

"He'll feel it. He has a way of knowing I don't understand."

"Well, where is he?"

"He's only fifteen minutes late," she said, glancing at her wristwatch and suddenly looking very tired. Their talk could not be intimate. The more lighthearted they tried to be, the more apparent it became they were both masking their concern. "The difficulty is," Mark began, "Jeremy is a very complicated intelligent man and he may be deliberately giving us a little time to say what we want to say to each other before he walks in on us with some easy excuse and charms us and we all embrace each other." Then, embarrassed, "You don't believe that? No. Hell, I don't know. Are you getting hungry?"

"I'm not hungry."

"We could go over to the hotel and have a good meal."

"No, we said we'd be here. Mark, I know he needs us to be here."

"You must know things I don't know," he said, trying to laugh.

Hurt by his laugh, she eyed him steadily, then suddenly changing, said, "Well, we're here anyway, aren't we? Just as we might be on another night in Paris." She sat with her arms folded. "There now," she said, "there's the scandalous Marta Sonbery coming in. She's all breasts and supposed to be an actress. And what about that little sculptress who's just had a baby, and tried to kill her lover. She looks prettier than ever, and who is going to be the new Pope?" Then, she blurted out, "What's happened to Jeremy? Where could he be?

Maybe he is letting us have a chance to talk. Maybe he's sitting at home. I'll see." She went into the café to telephone. Returning, she said, "No one answered. No one's there. I wonder if he's sound asleep. Anyway, I told you I was exhausted myself. Take me home, Mark."

Opening the apartment door, and before turning on the light, she called, "Jeremy," waiting and hoping to hear a voice before lighting up the rooms and seeing no one was there. She looked around for some sign that Jeremy had been there during the evening. Mark could only sit and watch her. After much pacing, she lay down on the couch, closing her eyes as if her worry had further exhausted her, and she murmured, "I'm glad you're here, Mark." Sitting beside her, watching the side of her face in the light from the lamp, he felt that for the first time they were really alone. In no time, she was asleep. Lightly, very lightly, he stroked her hair. His hand brushed over her breast. Her dress was high on her elegant leg. How little he knew her, he thought, so much of her unknown, so much to remain forever unknown, as it should be. The surprising freshness that came from her heart's core forever to be unknown. In Rome, or Paris, or Toronto, keeping her mystery. Then, he imagined he saw her as he had seen her in her apartment in Paris sitting on the couch, the cat beside her, but the cat had gone. Alfie was there instead of the cat. She was leaning forward, reaching out to his big dog, who stood there patiently. There was a beautiful serenity in her face. She was running her fingers lightly over Alfie's back. He kissed her lightly on the ear. His body, knowing something his mind did not understand, told him not to touch her now. Stretching out in the chair beside the bed, exhausted himself, he fell asleep and dreamt that Jeremy Monk had been seen in south Wales, and some said they had seen him at a festival in the highlands of Scotland.

They slept as they were till seven in the morning when they were awakened by two policemen pounding on the door. Jeremy Monk had been found this morning sitting on a bench under a gnarled squat tree in the Borghese Gardens, alone and dead. Clutched in his fist was an emptied vial of Valium tablets. Stuck prominently in the vest pocket of his jacket, a note: *Cretia, golden Cretia. As I said once to Mark about what I am doing now, don't worry. It's just like opening a door into another room.*